THE POWER OF HADES

THE HADES TRIALS

ELIZA RAINE

ROSE WILSON

Editors: Christopher Mitchell, Kyra Wilson, Brittany Smith

Cover: Kim's Covers

For everyone who is convinced that there's a goddess of hell inside them...

ONE

Blood. Everywhere I looked, there was blood. And fire. Flames were licking over the bodies where they lay motionless.

What have you done?

I tried to stagger to my feet but a wave of dizziness crashed over me and I dropped back to my knees. I didn't feel the pain as they cracked against the rocky ground, only saw the crimson blood as it splashed up my white dress.

What have you done?

'Persephone?' Someone was roaring my name and I turned, heat searing the skin on my face. 'Where are you?'

I made no noise. I didn't want him to find me. I couldn't let anyone find me. I couldn't face them all when they realized this was my fault. *I couldn't face him.* My gaze snagged on the body of a woman, only twenty feet from me. Her face was peaceful, even as her skin burned. Tears slid down my cheeks.

Look at what you've done to her. To them all.

Pain tore through my head, unbearable, as I heard him scream my name again. I couldn't live, while they burned.

TWO

'Persy? Isn't that a boy's name?'

I bit back a retort before it could slip from my lips, and forced them into a smile. Today was *not* the day I got sacked for swearing at a customer.

'Do you want milk in this Americano?' I asked the tall, muscular guy with the lopsided grin across the counter from me.

'Nah, I like my coffee bitter,' he said, and waggled his eyebrows at me. His gray eyes shone, and when I looked into them I found it strangely hard to look away again. I was sure I could see purple swirling around in them. 'So,' he said, pointing to my name badge. 'Parents wanted a boy?'

I sighed, snapping out of the pleasant effect his eyes were having on me.

'No. It's short for Persephone,' I said, slapping a plastic lid on the steaming coffee and sliding it over to him. 'Next!' I called.

'What time do you finish your shift? Are you busy later?' he said. I looked sideways at him as the next customer in the line, a doddery little old woman with a stick, stepped forward scowling.

'You need to move out the way,' I told him, and he bowed his head at the old lady apologetically. His pale hair flopped forward and he pushed his hand through it as he straightened, his chest muscles straining under his tight blue t-shirt.

'I'm so sorry, ma'am. I was just asking this delightful young lady if she had plans later this afternoon,' he smiled at her. I rolled my eyes as the lady's scowl vanished, replaced with a smile under flushing cheeks.

'Well, aren't you the lucky one,' she said to me.

'No, I'm not. I'm afraid I have plans this afternoon,' I said to the cocky guy.

'That's a shame,' he said, this time his smile not quite reaching his eyes and a wicked gleam forming in them instead. 'Catch you around, Persy,' he said, and strode from the coffee shop. A weird tingle skittered through me, and I shook my head as I turned back to the little old lady.

'I'd have canceled my plans if I were you,' she said, cheeks still pink. 'There aren't many men that look like that, even in New York.'

'In my experience, the prettiest men are the best ones to avoid,' I told her. 'Now, what can I get you?'

My shift at Easy Espresso lasted another two hours, and

even though a steady trickle of caffeine-starved customers kept me busy, I couldn't shift those mesmerizing eyes from my mind. I'd meant what I'd said though. Well-polished men whose second sentence was to ask you out were an absolute no-no for me. Unfortunately, my type was the effortlessly cool, ripped jeans, oily t-shirt, totally-distracted-by-something-stereo-typically-male-like-fixing-or-building-things guy. In short, the sort of guy who never, ever noticed or chatted up girls who worked in coffee shops.

I'd worked in Easy Espresso for a year now. I didn't hate it, but I didn't love it either. Don't get me wrong, working as a barista in a little, local coffee shop beat working in one of the big ones, where the lines were always ten people deep and everyone was angry and in a hurry. Easy Espresso had a more relaxed vibe, sand-wiched between a dry cleaners and a bakery, with only three little tables inside and the same outside. My boss, Tom, wasn't an asshole, which was rare for New York and a first for me, but I knew I wouldn't be there much longer. I only had one semester left at the New York Botanical Gardens, and when I graduated I'd be able to get a job doing what I really loved.

I felt a frisson of excitement as I shrugged on my biker jacket when Stacey arrived to take over from my shift at 2pm.

'See you tomorrow,' I called to her quickly, and raced though the door before she'd even got her ugly brown apron on. The crocuses should finally be opening in my little patch of greenhouse, and after Soil Science class I had a whole hour with Professor Hetz to go over the designs for my private garden. If I did a good enough job then he would put me forward for the landscape designer scholarship, and I'd actually have a shot at my dream career. And the way rooftop gardens were taking over the city, there was a good chance I could find enough work to stay in Manhattan too.

I grinned as I jogged towards the subway entrance, pulling my tatty slouch purse higher over my shoulder. The Botanical Gardens, and my beautiful domed lecture building, were in the Bronx, a good twenty minutes away, and I only had thirty minutes before Soil Science started. A flash of lightning caught my eye, and I cast my gaze upwards. Black clouds were rolling across the sky out of nowhere. *Weird.* It was forecast to be dry and warm all week, and after a dismally wet start to April, the city deserved some sunshine. People began to hurry around me, picking up their paces and scowling. I didn't have an umbrella and my little leather jacket wasn't going to keep much of me dry, so I upped my jog to a sprint, aiming for the cover of the subway underpass. A sudden clap of thunder made my heart leap in my chest, and I couldn't help slowing down to a stop and looking up at the sky again as the noise reverberated through the streets, bouncing off the towering buildings surrounding me. It had gotten dark quickly, and although there was still no rain falling, the sun was completely blocked by thick, dark clouds. I could see purple lightning sparking inside them, and then there was another crack of thunder. This one was so loud that an involuntary cry escaped my lips, my hands flying to my ears unbidden. Fear started to trickle through me. Outside in the city was no place to be during a lightning storm.

'You should get inside, Persy, where it's safe.' I jerked my gaze down from the lightning-filled clouds and my jaw dropped as I saw the blonde haired pretty-boy from earlier, standing ten feet away from me. And he was the only one on the streets, I realized, flicking my eyes from side to side. Where had everyone gone? There must have been fifty people bustling about not thirty seconds ago! *This was getting really fucking weird.* Panic was beginning to build inside me, and I took a step backwards. The pretty-boy smiled at me, then in the blink of an eye, he was standing directly in front of me.

I gasped, my pulse skyrocketing, and took another step back, but I couldn't take my eyes off his. Purple lightning was firing in his irises, in time with the flashes above me. It was utterly beautiful and completely terrifying. My muscles twitched as my heart hammered against my ribs. Every part of me wanted to get away from him, but I couldn't move.

'Who are you?' I breathed.

'You wouldn't believe me if I told you,' he grinned. 'But I don't like being turned down.'

A flicker of anger penetrated my fear. The pretty-boy couldn't take rejection? My mind filled with an image of Ted Hammond, who'd bullied me all through high school, making my life hell whilst anyone was looking, and worse when no one was.

'So you make flashy storms when girls aren't interested in you?' I raised my eyebrows at him. He laughed softly, and I swore he was starting to grow taller, beginning to loom over my already slight form. I instantly regretted what I'd said, the familiar helpless feeling making my insides shrink. *I wasn't strong enough to stop him.* It was the same thought that had dominated my life for years.

'Ohhhh, Persephone. I do so, so much worse than make flashy storms.' He was beginning to glow a faint purple, and I screamed as a bolt of lightning suddenly flashed from the sky, hitting him square on. Light erupted from him, and I turned and ran, my instincts finally taking hold of me. 'Where are you going, little Persy? There's no escaping me!' Booming laughter echoed around the empty streets, and my chest began to tighten, my lungs burning as I ran faster. I didn't know where I was going, panic blinding my ability to reason or think, an animalistic need to get away forcing my body to keep moving. Another purple flash blinded me momentarily and I skidded out of the way as a lightning bolt screeched down into the tarmac. The smell of burning asphalt filled my nostrils as I turned, spotting an entrance to the subway further up the abandoned street.

'Come on now, Persephone, Hades will be so upset with me if I fry you before I can get you to his realm.'

Hades? Did he just say Hades?

I kept running, my sneakers pounding the street, desperate to reach the subway. Lightning couldn't get underground, surely. But as I got closer the entrance to the subway shimmered, and my steps faltered as the world ahead of me morphed from 6th Avenue to a meadow, the subway entrance becoming a dark and gaping cave mouth. I stumbled hard and fell to one knee, landing on soft grass instead of hard asphalt. My breathing was shallow now, my mind reeling, and I scrabbled back to my feet and spun around. How the hell was this happening? *What* the hell was happening? A wave of dizziness swamped me as I tried to process the endless green turf and pretty flowers surrounding me.

'Where am I?' I shrieked, looking around for the lightning-eyed pretty-boy. Dark clouds still rolled overhead, flashing purple. 'Why am I here? Who the hell are you?' Tears of frustration and fear began to fill my eyes. I had a class to get to. I needed to show Professor Hetz my garden. The garden I'd worked on for months, that my whole future depended on... Some part of me knew that the garden should have been the least of my worries, but it had occupied every corner of my mind for months. It was a chance at a new start, where nobody would see me as weak or poor. I had to cling to something real in this twisted hallucination, or whatever the hell it was, and all I had was my garden.

There was another boom of thunder, and rain began to fall from the flashing clouds, heavy and cold. I let out a roar of anger, still turning around frantically, looking for the asshole who'd fucked my day up so tremendously.

'Where are you, you cowardly bastard?!' I screamed. As if in answer, the rain pelted down harder and lightning streaked towards the earth on every side of me.

THREE

At least ten streaks of lightning zigzagged into the earth in a ring around me, the light so bright my arms flew up instinctively to cover my drenched face. The screeching sound they made penetrated my skull so deeply I felt dizzy with fear. I had to get somewhere safe, somewhere the lightning couldn't get me. I blinked, trying to clear the light from my vision, but the only thing I could see in the empty meadow was the cave mouth. It was set into a little mound not more than three feet high, with stone steps leading down into the earth just barely visible in the darkness.

Surely that's where he wanted me to go? Which meant it was the last place I should be considering. Another boom of thunder echoed around me and my terrified body jumped in fright.

I couldn't stay where I was, I decided, and pushed my sodden hair back from my face as I ran for the cave.

I ducked low as I stepped into the darkness,

welcoming the instant relief from the rain. Panting from running and shouting, I sat down hard on the top step, looking out over the meadow as I tried to organize my crashing thoughts. My hands were shaking and my mouth felt dry, and I knew adrenaline was surging through me. *This couldn't be happening*, I asserted mentally, screwing my face up. I must have had some sort of nervous breakdown, or a stroke or something. Maybe I'd been hit by a car? Clearly a gorgeous guy who could control lightning hadn't just magicked me into a meadow and blasted electricity at me to get me to go into a cave. Clearly. Because that would be batshit crazy. Next-level crazy.

I took a deep breath, and began to wring out my long dark hair. It sure was wet for a hallucination. I patted my purse, though the gesture was more out of habit than anything useful. My cell phone had no battery. And who was I going to call anyway? I was probably lying on 6th Avenue unconscious, or with any luck in the back of an ambulance by now. Hopefully the medics would charge up my phone and find my brother's number. He would sort this out. Sam was good at sorting stuff out.

I took another long breath. I was starting to feel better. There was no way on earth this was real. I wasn't in a cave, in a meadow, being hounded by a man made of lighting. *I couldn't be*. And if this was all a dream then it couldn't hurt to take a look around. After all, if I was in a coma or some shit, then I might be here for a while. Channeling my new-found confidence through my body, I stood up, surprised at how shaky my hallucinated legs felt. And how cold my hallucinated skin was.

It's obviously a very intense hallucination, I thought, squinting into the darkness below me. Those happened all the time, didn't they?

I put a wobbly, wet sneaker out in front of me, and carefully took a step further into the cave, my socks squelching. Great. What were the chances of there being a laundromat at the bottom of these steps, I wondered? To be fair, if I was dreaming the whole thing, then probably quite high. Maybe I could conjure up some other nice things to be waiting for me at the bottom, I thought, taking another step into the darkness. Maybe a lemon drizzle cake. Or a series of hot guys in dirty overalls, and a shower big enough for them all.

Before long, I was ten steps down, and my eyes were adjusting to the lack of light. The stone steps were worn and uneven, so I was moving slowly, but they seemed to go on and on. After another ten minutes my fantasies about the filthy mechanics were struggling to occupy my mind. Down I went, desperately clinging to happy thoughts as the panic deep in my gut tried to crawl its way up into my throat. Where the hell was I going? I could swear it was getting warmer, although that could have been because I was drying off and moving. Or perhaps it was the anxiety making me hot. Anxiety always made me hot.

After what felt like an hour, but was probably closer to fifteen minutes of putting one soggy foot in front of another and moving deeper and deeper into the earth, I finally saw a flicker of light ahead of me. *Blue* light. I hurried my pace, still taking care on the dodgy steps, but keen to find out what in the world could be causing flickering blue light. Maybe it was the ambulance lights, wherever my body *really* was, leaking into my hallucination. My breathing quickened as the steps rounded a bend. Sconces lined the rocky walls at intervals, each holding a torch burning with blue fire.

'What the...' I murmured, holding my hand hesitantly up to one of them, and drawing it back quickly as I felt the fierce heat. Well, I thought, raising my eyebrows, impressed. Maybe my brain was capable of more imagination than I'd been giving it credit for. *I wonder what else is down here?*

I didn't have to go much further before the steps leveled out, turning into a long flat corridor lined with more torches. I walked faster once I was on safer ground, looking up at the tunnel roof periodically. I wasn't claustrophobic, but when underground it seemed sensible to check the earth above your head was stable once in a while. I walked for about a mile before I reached a closed wooden door, carved with what looked like ancient Greek letters, all glowing the same blue as the torches on the walls. I reached out for the iron ring in the middle and pulled hesitantly. The door didn't budge. I pulled harder, dreading the thought of having to go back up all those steps, back into the stormy meadow. The door didn't move even a millimeter, and I snarled as I dropped the ring in frustration. It thudded against the wood and then bounced twice, the knocks ringing out loudly in the narrow chamber. I froze, the noise unexpected and unnerving. A slow creak sounded, and I took a quick step back from the door. It was swinging open.

If I'd thought my imagination had done well with blue fire, then it deserved a freaking award for the woman stood in front of me.

She was pale-skinned and wearing skin-tight black leather from head to foot, showing a hell of a lot of cleavage. Jet black hair run through with hundreds of tiny tight silver plaits was pulled up in a high ponytail, which showed the intricate black pattern tattooed on the shaved bottom half of her skull. Silver jewelry covered her ears, wrists and hands, all of it sharp. Earrings like daggers hung down from her lobes, and she wore finger sheaths that ended in gleaming claw-like points. A shining tiara set with a single black stone was wrapped around her forehead, which drew attention to her most remarkable feature of all. *She had no pupils.* Her eyes were pure white.

'Welcome to hell,' she said, with a grin.

FOUR

As I watched, too stunned to do anything else, the white began to leak from her eyes, and her grin slipped as electric blue irises and dark pupils began to form.

'No. Fucking. Way,' she said slowly. I moved my mouth but no words came out. I just gaped at her, and she gaped back. 'He found you. He actually fucking found you. Oh gods, Hades is gonna... Oh shit. Oh shit, shit, shit!' She stamped her foot, her silky voice rising in pitch and her hands flexing into fists.

'Who found me?' I half-whispered. 'And... why is everyone talking about Hades?'

The woman chewed on her bottom lip as her black brows drew together. She shook her head.

'Zeus. Zeus found you. I don't believe it.'

I let out a barked laugh and she leaned one hand on her hip, unsmiling.

'It's not funny, it's a fucking disaster.'

'What are you talking about? And who are you?' I said, my confidence growing at her words. I'd been obsessed with Greek mythology since I was a kid. This was *definitely* something my stupid-ass brain would make up.

'I'm Hecate. And you're Persephone. And you're not supposed to be here, that's what I'm talking about.'

'Hecate? As in the goddess of magic?'

'Amongst other things, yeah,' she said, regarding me. 'So... you remember some stuff then?'

'From classical studies? Yeah, I remember loads,' I said, frowning. 'I carried on studying Greeks and Romans after school.'

'Classical studies. Right,' Hecate said, nodding slowly. 'You remember nothing from...' she trailed off, raising one perfect eyebrow at me. I raised both of mine back at her.

'What are you talking about?' I said eventually, when she didn't speak. She blew out a sigh.

'Hades is going to lose it when he sees you. But I guess that's what you get for pissing off the Lord of the Gods. Fucking idiot.'

'Hades is a fucking idiot?'

'Yeah. But for the sake of the gods, don't say that in front of him. Or tell him I said it.'

'I had no idea I was this imaginative,' I breathed.

'What?'

'This isn't happening,' I told her. 'I've invented you.'

A lopsided smile took over her face, and her blue eyes twinkled.

'Is that right?'

'Must be,' I said. 'Zeus and Hades and Greek gods don't exist. I'm sure we'd have noticed by now if they did.' Even as I spoke the words, doubt and panic were warring with them. Something was wrong, Very, very wrong. *That'll be the fact that you're probably gravely injured or dying somewhere in the real world*, I reminded myself.

'You've been in the mortal realm a long time, Persephone,' said Hecate, quietly.

'New York,' I told her. 'And I've been there twenty-six years. *My whole life.*' I stressed the last sentence.

'Sure you have,' she said, in a voice that said I was totally deluded. 'What the fuck am I supposed to do with you now?'

'Well, you were obviously expecting someone,' I said, thinking back to her white eyes. 'You welcomed me to hell.'

'Yeah, I was expecting the last contestant for the Hades Trials. I just didn't expect it to be you.'

'The Hades Trials?'

'You know, for someone who's made all this up in their head, you have very little clue about what's going on,' Hecate said. She had a point. My stomach lurched uneasily again.

'So why don't you tell me?' I put my hands on my hips in an attempt to regain some sort of semblance of control, but the woman in front of me was clearly a hundred times more fierce than I could ever be.

'OK. Zeus has decided that Hades needs a wife. Women have been trying to earn the position of Queen of the Underworld by completing a series of Trials. I was supposed to meet the last contestant here today.'

'Can Hades not just choose someone he likes?' I asked, frowning at my own question. This was absolutely mad.

'No. He swore after his first wife that he would never remarry, but he upset Zeus in a pretty big way recently. And the big man's punishments cut deep.'

'Hades is being forced to marry as a punishment?'

'Yep.'

'So... what's this all got to do with me? And how do you know who I am?'

A worried look crossed her beautiful face, then she let out a big sigh and closed her eyes.

'What a fucking mess,' she breathed, and opened her eyes again, fixing them on mine. 'I could refuse to tell you, but I guess you'll find out sooner or later.'

'Find what out?'

'You're Hades' first wife.'

My head swam for a moment as I gaped at her. Then a laugh, bordering on hysterical, bubbled from my lips, getting louder and louder as the words repeated themselves in my head.

'How the hell am I coming up with this?' I gasped through laughs. 'I've made myself the wife of the king of the dead? What the actual fuck?' Fresh laughter welled out of me, my ribs starting to ache as I leaned over, pressing my hands on my knees. 'I mean, there's being into bad boys, but Hades? Lord of the Underworld? Talk about extreme!'

'This is so not how I saw today going,' sighed Hecate. She let me laugh a while longer, tears streaming from my eyes as adrenaline-fueled instability took over my senses. 'Are you done?' she asked, when the laughter began to ebb away, and I dabbed at my wet cheeks. I nodded.

'I'm so done. Done with all of this. I need to wake up now.'

'Persephone, this isn't a dream,' she said, stepping forward and gripping my arm hard.

'Ow!' I exclaimed, my laughter dying out abruptly.

'See? You can feel that?'

'Yes,' I said sharply, tugging my arm back.

'This is real. And trust me when I tell you, you don't want to fuck with Zeus or Hades. Or any of the Olympians for that matter. If Zeus found you and brought you here, then you have to compete in the Trials. And that has... ramifications.'

I scowled at her.

'No. No, I'm sorry.' I turned, and my stomach lurched as I bumped into a wall made from solid earth. 'Where's the corridor gone?' I asked, my voice weak. Blue light flared around me and I spun back to Hecate. Her eyes were milky white again and her hands were raised by her face. Thin wisps of purple smoke were trailing from her palms, and slowly they convalesced into a dagger, spinning gently in the air in front of me. I felt my heart begin to hammer in my chest. 'I need to sit down,' I said, feeling my legs wobble beneath me.

'Persephone, you have a past in this realm. A past I am not at liberty to divulge.' Her voice had gone weirdly formal, compared to how she'd been speaking before. 'But I can tell you that Hades will be very shocked, and very angry to see you. And there will be many others who will be less than pleased. This weapon will work here in Olympus, even on a god, and you should keep it on you at all times.'

The dagger floated towards my shaking hands, and I tentatively reached for it. It was warm to touch, and had a little green stone set in each side of the pommel. Other than that it was unremarkable.

'Thanks,' I muttered, staring at it. It felt real in my grasp. *Too real.* I squeezed my eyes closed. *Wake up, wake up, wake up. Sam, where the fuck are you? Wake me up!*

Nothing happened. That didn't mean anything though. There was no way I was the wife of Hades. I'd been watching too much Netflix.

But something in my core was straining, almost longing for this craziness to be true. *Why? Why would I want that?* In what world would I want to compete to be the wife of a god I had apparently already been married to once, then completely forgotten? I wanted to design gardens! I wanted to grow living things! I didn't want to be in a cave with a magic dagger and angry gods!

'I want to go home,' I whispered, looking at Hecate. 'I was going to have a meeting today about my scholarship.'

A flicker of pity flashed across Hecate's face, her eyes blue again.

'I'm sorry,' she said quietly. 'Zeus is a prick. Don't tell him I said that either.'

'Can you send me back?'

She shook her head sadly.

'For your sake and Hades, I wish I could. But there's no crossing the big man.' She cocked her head at me again. 'You know, deep down, that this is real, don't you?'

I looked at her.

'I know something is wrong,' I admitted.

'Maybe when you see the realm, some of it will come back to you. Hopefully not all of it,' she added quietly. I frowned.

'If what you're saying is true, why will Hades be angry to see me? Did we fall out?'

'Something like that. Only he can tell you what happened. And he will likely choose not to.'

'Why?'

'Persy, I can't tell you, so don't ask, alright?' she said, a flicker of exasperation in her tone.

'Persy?'

She gave me an apologetic look.

'Sorry. That's what I used to call you. Before you... left.'

'Were we friends?'

'Yeah. You had cooler hair then. And much better dress sense.'

I looked down at my leather jacket and ripped jeans, then at her sleek black catsuit.

'Oh,' I said, not sure what else to say. My brain seemed to have slowed down completely, almost like it was refusing to process anymore. 'I can't think straight,' I told Hecate. 'And I feel very tired suddenly.'

'Let's get you some food and dry clothes. Maybe a stiff drink. The gods know, I need one,' she said and held out her hand.

I paused for a second, then took it.

FIVE

I followed Hecate through the wooden door and down more corridors lit with blue flames. They reflected off her silver jewelry and I let the light and patterns they made occupy my frazzled mind as we walked. I figured there was no point trying to concentrate on where we were going if walls could just appear to block the way. There was no point concentrating on anything really. This whole mad situation seemed to be far beyond my control. I was unbelievably tired and I wondered if going to sleep in this pretend place might make me wake up in the real world.

'Technically I'm supposed to present you to the gods in an hour, but I'll let them know we'll be a bit late,' Hecate said over her shoulder to me. 'Zeus won't be surprised, the asshole,' she snarled.

'Why did he come and find me?'

'I already told you, because it'll upset Hades.'

'Oh yeah. Apparently my ex-husband hates me.' I rolled my eyes. *Batshit crazy*.

'Woah now, I never said that,' she said, slowing down and looking back at me.

'You did too!'

'No, I said he'll be angry to see you. You're not supposed to be here.'

'Right. Is this one of those messy divorce things?' I asked with a sigh. None of this made any sense.

'Hmm, something like that. There'll need to be some damage limitation. I'll do what I can but...' She trailed off. She didn't speak again until we reached another door covered in glowing blue marks, which I was now positive were Greek. 'Persy, this is going to be a bit weird for you. Don't freak out on me, OK? Just... act normal.'

I looked at her.

'I'm too tired to freak out,' I told her. It was true. My thoughts were becoming more and more sluggish, and my legs felt like they weighed a ton. The adrenaline was wearing off. 'Plus I have no idea what normal is here,' I pointed out. 'I don't even know where I am.'

'You're in Olympus. Virgo, to be precise.'

'Virgo? Like the star sign?'

'Each of the Olympians has their own realm, and yeah, in your world they're star signs. Hades' realm is Virgo.'

'My star sign is Capricorn,' I said. 'Who's realm is that?'

'Artemis. And she and Hades do not get on. Also her realm is forbidden, except if you're a centaur. So unless you're hiding a horse body under those jeans, give up any ideas of visiting.'

'Right,' I said. Centaurs. Of course there were centaurs here. A little surge of panic bit through my fatigue. This couldn't be happening. *But it was.* At least there was something about Hecate I trusted. *Likely because she was a figment of my own imagination and I'd invented her for exactly that reason.* I would just try to treat anything and anyone in this place as though it were completely ordinary, I decided firmly. What other choice did I have? Freaking out wouldn't do me any good at all. As long as I could do nothing about this messed up situation, I might as well go along with it.

The room on the other side of the door was not that weird after all. It was a bit like a dressing room, with rails of clothes down one side, and a long counter down the other, with a mirror above it. The light wasn't blue anymore though, the rocky walls giving off a pale glow closer to daylight.

'Is all of Virgo underground?' I asked, then immediately wished I hadn't. I didn't expect to be here long, but I seriously couldn't handle being in a place where there was no outside. Panic fluttered through me, threatening to derail my new attitude adjustment.

'Not all of it, no,' Hecate said, bending to open a cupboard under the counter. She straightened and handed me a straight cut glass. She held onto one herself and I watched as her eyes turned milky. Red liquid began to fill her glass, and I looked down to see the same happening in mine.

'What is it?'

'Wine,' she said as the blue returned to her irises.

'You can conjure wine? I'd be drunk constantly,' I said, impressed. She winked at me.

'Who says I'm not?' She knocked back a huge gulp of the liquid, and I hesitantly lifted my glass to my lips and inhaled. It smelled divine, like black currants and cherries. I took a sip.

'Wow,' I said, involuntarily. Hecate gave me a look, pursing her lips.

'I'm actually quite jealous that you get to discover Olympus all over again. The first time you do anything is always the best,' she sighed.

'And you can't tell me why I left in the first place?'

'No. I'm not even sure myself, but even if I was, Hades would kill me.' She flicked her hand, eyes flashing white again, and a chocolate cake appeared out of nowhere on the counter, in front of the mirror. My stomach growled in response.

'Can you do anything you like with your magic?' I asked her.

'I can do quite a lot,' she shrugged, steering me towards a chair in front of the mirror. 'But it's not all fun and games. I'm also goddess of ghosts. That's a lot less fun, I can tell you.'

'Really?' I asked, as she sat me down and stood behind me. I watched in the mirror as she lifted a lock of my dark, wet hair and let it fall back onto my jacket with a slapping sound.

'Yeah. Most folk aren't exactly thrilled to find their souls stuck as corporeal beings. Sometime it feels like I'm wading though shit trying to sort out their messes.'

'Is that why you live in the underworld? Because of the ghosts?'

'Uhuh. Now, we need to do something about your hair. And eat some cake. You'll feel better.'

I thought about refusing, remembering something about not eating food from the underworld, but the cake looked and smelled amazing. This whole place is pretend, I reminded myself, and lifted a slice from the cake. What harm could it possibly do? I took a bite, sensations firing in my mouth as the richest chocolate I'd ever tasted slid over my tongue.

'Oh my god,' I mumbled around the cake.

'Gods,' Hecate corrected me. 'Twelve of them. And don't forget it.'

'Right,' I nodded. I looked at her in the mirror as she rummaged though the rails of clothes behind me.

'I'm not wearing something like...' I trailed off as she straightened and raised one eyebrow.

'Like what?'

'Like what you are,' I finished awkwardly. 'You look great in it! But I'm not quite as... confident about the bust area as that outfit requires.'

'Persy, from what I remember, that's a load of shit. But don't worry, I was planning on something a little more conservative. If you went out in front of Hades in skin-tight leather he might bust something,' she said, frowning at a green dress on a hanger. I shook my head. Maybe when I met my alleged ex-husband this would start to make more sense. Maybe not. I finished the piece of cake and glugged down the rest of the wine, already starting to feel much more alert.

'So, tell me about the Trials,' I said. 'What will I have to do?'

'Er, best you find that out later,' she answered evasively. Alarm trickled through me. *It doesn't matter, it's not real,* I told myself.

'Are they dangerous?'

Hecate shrugged.

'There've been a few casualties,' she said, sliding a pale blue thing off a hanger.

'What?' I said, spinning on my chair to face her. 'Casualties? What kind of casualties?'

'Don't worry about it, with any luck Hades will find a way to withdraw you anyway,' she smiled at me, but I knew she was lying. I took a deep breath.

'I like the green,' I said, pointing at the dress still on the rail.

'Oh. OK.'

'And can I have some more wine?'

'Hecate, why is my hair white?' I kept my voice as level as I could, but it flickered all the same. 'I've dealt with enough weird shit today, and I'm not sure I can add this to the list.'

'Shush, you've not seen it all together yet. You look amazing.'

She'd hidden the mirror from me, turning it a smoky black, but I could see the lock of my hair that had fallen over my shoulder and was now laying across my left breast. The pale green dress was a halterneck, showing only a moderate amount of cleavage, but it was tight around my waist. The bottom half of the dress flowed like liquid to the floor though, shimmering turquoise when I moved, and a thigh-high split showed the off the gold lace-up sandals on my now-dry feet.

If it weren't for the little piece of white hair dominating my attention, I would have been quite thrilled with the outfit.

'OK, are you ready?'

'Do I have a choice?'

'Nope. Ta da!'

The mirror cleared, and my mouth fell open. My hair was *white*. Not like when an old person goes gray, but white. I moved my head from side to side and saw silvery strands catch the light. It was set in gentle curls and half tied up, with lots of little plaits everywhere like Hecate's. A few stray curls fell about my ears, brushing my bare shoulders. I leaned closer to peer at my reflection. My green eyes looked more green somehow, like fresh grass, dark liner rimming them and making them pop. A deep purple colored my lips, making them look fuller, and my cheekbones looked sharper too.

'What have you... How did you make me look so...' I couldn't finish any of the sentences. I looked a thousand times better than I had ever managed to make myself look.

Hecate beamed at me.

'Just wait until I get you into some of your old dresses,' she said, eyes flashing. 'Although we'll need some fighting gear too.'

'Fighting?' I raised my eyebrows. 'Other than scrapping with my big brother, I'm not really a fighter. I'm more of the 'love things, grow things', type of gal.'

'I'm sure it'll all come back.' I opened my mouth, but shut it again. There was no point in asking her what that meant. I was just going to go along with this. 'OK. I think you're ready. Finish that wine and we'll go.'

I downed the rest of my drink in one, and rolled my shoulders as I stood up.

'I'm ready,' I told her and she took my hand in hers.

'Good. I'm sorry.'

'For what?'

'This,' she said, and her eyes turned milky.

SIX

The world around me lurched, white light flashing bright around me. I squeezed my eyes closed and gripped Hecate's hand harder, then I heard the muttering of a crowd, which died away almost instantly. I opened my eyes.

'Oh my god,' I whispered.

I was in a white marble room, facing tiered rows of seated people. And the word 'people' was a loose description. Although over half of them looked human, a lot didn't. There was a woman with a severely misshapen face and leathery wings protruding from her back, and a beautiful lady whose skin looked like it was made from wood. There was a man who must have been ten feet tall if he had been stood up, his skin a shining gold color, and a creature that had furry legs that looked like a cat's and a beak for a nose. Standing at the back, just in front of the white marble wall were three minotaurs, a centaur and an incredibly curvy woman with a wooden leg and hair that seemed to be moving of its own accord. I took a deep breath. *OK. Ten, no, make that a hundred points, to my imagination.*

'I did warn you,' muttered Hecate, still gripping my hand. As I turned to look at her I realized that the sides of the room were missing, grand Greek columns lining the edges at intervals instead. And beyond them were flames. And not just any flames. Flames larger than sky-scrapers that leapt and danced and weren't only red. Purples and blues and oranges flickered amongst the crimson and I was vaguely aware of my jaw slowly dropping.

'It's so beautiful,' I breathed.

'Welcome to the Underworld,' boomed a voice.

I turned to the last wall and my knees instantly felt weak again. I was in a throne room, I now realized. There was a raised dais at the end of the room, and eleven people were seated on large chairs along the platform. These weren't people though, I knew, as my eyes flicked across them all, trying to take it in. *These were gods.* Power emanated from them, almost tangible in the air, as they each eyed me.

'It's really not Zeus's place to welcome you here,' said the most beautiful woman I'd ever seen, sitting forward in her chair. 'That honor should go to Hades, but he is... indisposed just now.' She had skin the color of coffee, and her hair was pastel pink and wrapped around her body like a dress, leaving her midriff and long legs totally exposed. Her pale lips matched her hair and her eyes were almost black. 'I'm Aphrodite,' she said.

I gazed at her, all the liquid leaving my mouth completely. Hecate squeezed my hand.

'Bow,' she said out of the corner of her mouth. I dipped my head low, taking another breath.

Get a grip, get a grip.

'I'm-' I started to say as I straightened, but a man stood up, cutting me off.

'You're Persephone,' he said, his eyes gleaming and purple energy crackling around him.

'You!' I said, anger springing to life inside me. He was Zeus! With his stupid purple lightning, and asshole laughing eyes.

'Me!' he beamed, his dark beard and hair morphing into that of the gorgeous blonde from the coffee shop. 'I'm ever so pleased you could join us,' he said. 'Some quick introductions? It would be rude for you to remain ignorant.' I glared at him, but kept my lips pressed firmly together. This was not the place to pick a fight, even I could tell that.

'This is my brother, Poseidon,' he said, gesturing to a bored-looking man with insanely blue eyes in the seat next to him. 'And this is my lovely wife, Hera.' The grand looking lady on the other side of him inclined her head at me and I returned the nod. She had inky dark skin and turquoise blue hair in a complicated looking plait that ringed her head like a crown. She had a real crown too, glittering with the reflections of the flames on either side of us.

'These are the twins, Artemis and Apollo,' he said, pointing at two slight, golden-haired figures, both sporting broad smiles. Artemis looked no older than fifteen, her brother maybe only a few years older. 'This is Dionysus.' Zeus gestured at a man dressed in clothes from my world, tight leather trousers and a Hawaiian shirt open to his navel. Dionysus gave me a lazy grin from under a flop of dark hair.

'Nice to see you again, Persy,' he drawled. I blinked thickly at him.

'This is Hermes,' Zeus said, and a red-headed man with a neat beard beamed at me. I couldn't help the small smile that leapt to my lips in return. There was something about him that slightly eased my racing pulse. 'You've just met Aphrodite, this is her husband, Hephaestus.' A man with a hunched shoulder and lopsided face was sat next to Aphrodite, his form swamped by a massive leather tabard. He didn't look at me. 'And this is Ares and Athena,' Zeus finished. An enormous man in full Greek armor glared at me through the eye-slit in his red-plumed helmet, and a beautiful blonde-haired woman in a white toga with an owl on her shoulder gave me a small smile. Athena had always been my favorite growing up. She was portrayed in my books as the goddess who was the most fair and most intelligent, but still fierce, and I'd tried to channel that every time Ted Hammond had got too close to me. *Not that I'd ever been able to stand up to him*, I thought bitterly. Even sat next to Ares' hulking form, Athena radiated power greater than his, and a respectful jealousy surged through me.

I bowed my head.

'It's nice to meet you all. I must confess though, I'm a little confused,' I said, as formally as I could, my lips slightly numb. 'Apparently you all know me from a life I can't remember.'

Athena stood up from her chair and my skin prickled with something, magic or power or anticipation, I wasn't sure.

'Persephone, you have been made to forget your past with good reason. It is highly inappropriate that you are here now, but there's nothing we can do about it. The Lord of the Gods has made sure of that.' She shot a sideways glare at Zeus, who flopped back into his throne with a lazy shrug.

'Oops,' he said.

'I know this may be hard for you, but you need to act as though this is your first time here in Olympus.'

'Erm, that's not going to be hard for me,' I said. 'I've never seen this place or any of you before in my life.'

'You misunderstand me. You will want to find out what happened in your past. But this would be folly. You must trust that the twelve Olympians made the correct decision in removing those memories from you, and leave it at that. Start again. From today.'

I frowned, confusion and anger battling against the compulsion I felt to worship this beautiful, wise woman. I knew hazily that her powers were at work. I mean, she was a goddess, she could make me do whatever she wanted. But was it right that they could remove my memories? Tell me I was married, then not allow me to know any more? *Married!* The thought was laughable. I'd never even had a boyfriend for more than six months, what the hell would I want with a husband? *None of this is real, you idiot. Who gives a shit?* The voice trickled through my racing thoughts. *Sam is going to wake you up soon, in a hospital bed somewhere.*

I smiled at Athena.

'Fine,' I said. She cocked her head at me slowly.

'You do not believe this is real?'

I said nothing and the goddess let out a long breath.

'Father, you can be cruel,' she said quietly, then sat back down on her throne.

'If Hades didn't behave like a disobedient child then I wouldn't have to be,' Zeus barked.

'And her? Do you believe she deserved this?' said Hera, speaking for the first time and gesturing at me. Zeus shifted uncomfortably in his seat.

'You forget, brother, she has the potential to be dangerous. Your games should not go this far,' said Poseidon, his piercing blue eyes not leaving me as he spoke.

'Dangerous?' I echoed.

'Dangerous,' he repeated, something in his expression making me want to be someplace else, and fast.

'I will be her companion during the Trials, she will not be a danger to anyone,' said Hecate, stepping forward beside me. Relief and gratitude washed through me as I remembered I wasn't completely alone. Hecate had been my friend once, apparently.

'Hmmm. To be sure, I wish to assign her a guard. Of

my choosing,' said Poseidon, finally taking his eyes from mine and looking at Zeus.

'I would like to choose a guard for her too,' said Athena quickly.

'As I'm sure would Hades, were he here,' added Hera.

Zeus rolled his eyes and sighed, and I looked at Hecate.

'Why the fuck do I need a guard?' I hissed at her.

'Her powers haven't been unlocked,' said Hecate loudly to the assembled gods, ignoring me. 'She does not need a guard.'

'Powers?' I gaped at her, feeling the hysteria fringing my mind again. *Of course I'd give myself powers in this mad fucking fantasy. Why wouldn't I?* 'Let me guess,' I said, feeling an unhinged smile take over my face. *If I could have any power in the world what would it be?* That was easy. 'I can make plants grow?'

Hecate looked at me, her brows drawing together.

'How'd you know that?'

'Because Hades left her love of nature when he sent her to the mortal world,' said Hera, so quietly I barely heard her.

A silence fell over the room and my head span as the colored flames danced on each side of us.

'I suggest Persephone choose her own guard. We will present our options this evening, after the first Trial,' said Athena, authoritatively.

'Agreed,' said Zeus, sitting forward. 'Now, I do not believe Hades will be joining us now-'

'And why is that, brother?' boomed a voice. Goose-flesh shot up on my skin as the temperature in the room dropped sharply. Fear began to crawl through me, though I didn't know what I was suddenly so scared of. I felt Hecate stiffen by my side and Zeus's eyes flashed as he slouched back into his throne.

'Hades! I'm so glad you could make it after all! I have a surprise for you.'

Black smoke began to gather in the center of the dais, swirling fast into a humanoid form.

'Another contestant for your foolish competition, no doubt,' hissed the angry, slithery voice, and I felt a strong compulsion to step backwards, and keep going.

'Indeed,' said Zeus, a smile spreading over his face. The smoke was nearly solid now, but not quite, the form before me translucent and fluid and featureless.

Until it turned to me.

For a split second the world disappeared completely. The first thing I saw were his eyes, the rest of the swirling smoke flashing into human form so briefly I almost missed it. But I registered the massive shoulders, the dark trousers and shirt, the gleaming onyx in the center of a belt around his waist, before my eyes met his again. *They were silver.* Not white or grey or pale blue but shining silver, and they were filled with shock. Emotions I didn't recognize began to hammer through me, and suddenly something inside me was beating against my mind, desperate to be free. The sensation made me feel dizzy and sick.

I knew this man. All notion of this being a crazy dream, all ideas that I was hallucinating, all the rational thoughts and truths that I'd been clinging to disintegrated as I stared into those desperate pools of silver. I knew this man. *This was real.*

Anger suddenly erupted in those haunted eyes and before I could look at the rest of his face his solid form was gone. A blast of power pulsed through the room and I cried out as pure terror gripped my mind. Images that were usually relegated to my worst nightmares, blood and death and gore and fire, filled my head and blinded me to everything else. I could smell the tang of the blood, hear the fire roaring, feel the screams reverberating around me as people died everywhere I looked. *I was drowning in blood.* I choked for breath as my legs crumpled beneath me, too far gone to feel the crack of my knees as they hit the marble.

'What is the meaning of this?' bellowed Hades, so loudly I threw my hands over my ears, squeezing my eyes shut. It didn't help. All I could see were bodies, torn apart, flames licking over them. I clawed at my throat desperately, unable to get enough air. *I was drowning in fear and blood.*

'Hades!' I distantly heard Hecate's voice. 'She doesn't have her power, you're going to kill her!'

Instantly the terror melted away, a soothing calm flooding through me. I gulped down air, pressing my shaking hands to my wet face as Hecate crouched down beside me.

'It's OK,' she said quietly. 'You'll be OK.'

'Everybody, leave,' the slithery voice said. Although he spoke quietly, the words were as clear as day. 'Except you, brother. You and I need to talk.'

SEVEN

Hecate had barely magicked us out of the throne room and I was still clinging to her arm as the combination of terror and adrenaline finally got the better of me and my stomach began to heave.

'Red wine and chocolate cake is not so appealing anymore,' muttered Hecate, staring down in distaste at the mess I'd made on the dressing room floor. Then there was a fizzing sound, and the vomit vanished. 'Here,' she said, handing me a glass of water. I took it with shaking hands and she eased me onto the stool. 'I've never seen Hades lose control of his power like that. I'm sorry.'

'What's his power, scaring people to death?' I asked, my voice coming out in a bitter croak.

'Well, no, but that is an unfortunate side-effect for humans.'

'Huh.' I took a long shuddering breath.

'I saw... I saw horrible things,' I said quietly.

'Dead people?' she asked, quirking an eyebrow, her braids flashing as she cocked her head at me. I nodded.

'Yeah. Lots of dead people.'

'Hades is the Lord of the Dead. He's the most fearsome of all the Olympians, although not the strongest, and his rage would cause any human to see death. And trust me, that was Hades' real rage.' She blew out a breath, chewing on her lip. 'He let his true form show. With spectators. That's... Well, there are very, very few people in Olympus who have seen his eyes.'

Those silver orbs, deep with desperation and power filled my mind.

'I know him,' I said quietly, looking down at my glass.

'Yes,' said Hecate, and crouched in front of me, her blue eyes full of compassion.

'But... My life. My life in New York...'

My real life felt distant in my spinning head, like it had just been a game, or a dream. I could feel it slipping away. Was that because I was dying somewhere in New York? Would this all end soon too? Or was this the reality? *Hades' eyes...* I knew, more surely than I'd ever known anything in my life, that this was not the first time I'd seen those eyes. They meant something to me, down to my very core. But what? Was it love for a husband? It didn't feel like love. And how the hell could I have loved someone whose power was to fill people's minds with scenes from their nightmares?

'I'm sorry your first meeting with him turned out like that. I knew it would be pretty shit but... Nearly killing you was definitely not ideal. But you have to trust me when I tell you that I think this could all work out OK. Maybe. If you're a fast learner and we can stop you being so... human.'

I blinked at Hecate.

'Right,' I said eventually, at a loss for anything more constructive.

'There's got to be a way of unlocking your powers, but we'll need to do it slowly. And without whichever stupid guard you end up with knowing about it.' She jumped to her feet. 'You want to hope you get either Athena's or Hades' guard, Poseidon's will be a total fucking killjoy.'

'Why does he think I'm dangerous?'

'Persy, we're back to shit I can't tell you, so stop asking.'

'Stop asking?' A flash of anger bubbled through my fatigue. 'Are you serious?'

'Look, this is what Athena meant. You have to accept that the past is in the past, and that's that.'

I glared at her, feeling a frisson of satisfaction as the confident look on her face flickered. I didn't think I'd ever intimidated anyone in my life before. But then I'd never looked or felt like this before either.

'I've been kidnapped, told my whole life was a lie and that I had a husband I didn't know existed. If that isn't bad enough, you now want me to compete to marry the same man who already decided NOT to be married to me once before, in order to live in a world full of dead things when all I've wanted to do my whole life is grow things.'

I stood up from the stool, aware of the increasing

pitch and volume of my voice and not caring one bit. 'How the fuck do you expect me not to ask you questions?'

'Calm down,' Hecate said quietly.

'Calm down? Are you insane? Of course you are! You live in hell and can conjure wine, why the fuck am I even talking to you?' I wheeled around, squeezing my eyes closed and pressing my hands to my face again. I was close to losing it, and I could feel the panic squeezing my chest. 'I'm not doing the Trials. I don't want to be here. I don't want anything to do with a creature who is surrounded by death, who *embodies* death.' Tears were burning the back of my eyes, and I squeezed them shut tighter. 'This is a fucking nightmare, please, let me out. Let me leave.' I didn't know who I was asking, I just desperately wanted the plea to come true. 'I can't stay here.' This was worse than school. This was worse than being taunted and called trailer trash and having stupid shit thrown at me. This was worse than Ted Hammond breathing down my neck, pawing and groping at me. Those bodies on fire, the smell of the blood, the paralyzing fear...

'I'm sorry, Persephone. You have to compete.' Hecate's voice sounded strained and sad behind me. 'I'm going to send you to sleep now. I'll wake you before the first Trial.'

'No, please-' I said, whipping around to face her, but I lost consciousness before she even came into view.

∾

I blinked and the world around me came blearily into view. I was in a bed, on a soft mattress, and a thick downy comforter was weighing down on me, covering my whole head. It felt cozy rather than smothering though, and I gripped it in my hands and wrapped it tighter around myself as the memories of the last few hours crashed over me like a wave. A hard lump formed in my throat as realization settled heavy within my heart. Now that the panic, the adrenaline, the mild hysteria was temporarily at bay, I knew with one hundred percent certainty that when I sat up and swung my legs out of bed, I would still be in this fucked up reality instead of my own. I knew this was real. As unlikely as it was, something deep in my core, maybe even in my soul if I had such a thing, knew it.

'Shit,' I muttered. 'Shit, shit, shit.' What would I do now? I thought about Athena's words. I was supposed to let go and move on. Hecate said I had to compete in the Trials. To marry the Lord of the Underworld. I shuddered. I couldn't marry that monster. No fucking way. I mean, he was made of smoke for Christ's sake! Those deep silver eyes shimmered into my mind.

You were married to him once. How? How was that even possible? I couldn't have loved him. He was freaking terrifying. And although I didn't consider myself as a total wimp, I wasn't exactly the sadist type, into blood and torture. My mind flashed to what sex with a man made of smoke and death would be like. Probably significantly more kinky than I was used to. *Stop it,* I chided myself.

All I had to do was not win the Trials. Then I

wouldn't have to marry him. And in all probability, I wouldn't be winning anything anyway. What would happen after I lost the Trials? Would I stay here in this world? Or get to go back to New York? I supposed either would be better than staying in the underworld. Did they employ gardeners in Olympus?

I lay still in the bed, refusing to peek out from the covers as I weighed up my options. One thing I kept coming back to was that panic and denial were unlikely to do me much good. If I had to fight, as Hecate had suggested I would, then I might face danger. Which meant being strong. Something I wasn't especially good at. I was good at avoiding fights, not getting into them. But I didn't want to be an easy target, not because mom and dad couldn't afford a house this time, but because I was human, and weaker than everyone else. I couldn't deal with that. Not again. It had taken six years to reach a point where I felt I could hold my own in New York. Six years to build up the confidence to follow my dreams, and actually make progress. Six years to reach a point where I could confidently turn down arrogant pretty-boys when they sleazed on me. Zeus's face filled my mind, merging with Ted Hammond's, and I scowled. No way was that happening again I thought, screwing my face up into the pillow, defiance buoying me. No fucking way.

Hecate said I used to have good dresses. And powers. I doubted I was ever as badass as she clearly was, but Poseidon had called me dangerous. Maybe instead of worrying about what had happened I should take Athena's advice, and forget about finding out what had occurred in the past and move on - become a new kind of dangerous. A new Persy, whom none of them wanted to fuck with. Especially that purple-eyed asshole, Zeus.

'Knock, knock?' came a questioning voice at the door, and I took a deep breath.

'Yeah?' I called, and reluctantly pulled the comforter from over my head.

'Good, you're up,' said Hecate, walking into the room through a massive mahogany door. I was in a windowless room, the walls all painted a rich navy blue and the ceiling giving off that same daylight glow that the dressing room walls had. I looked about, taking in the old-fashioned but expensive-looking wardrobe and dressing table, and the cabinet lined with glass bottles of colored liquids.

'Is that a bar?'

'Yes.'

'Good,' I said, and kicked the covers off. I made my way over to the grand little cabinet and poured some amber liquid from a square decanter into one of the two empty glasses.

'Do you want to know what that is before you drink it?' asked Hecate, but I shook my head, and tipped it down my throat. It burned, and my eyes began to water, but it was exactly what I needed. Fire in my belly, I thought, breathing through my teeth. I needed fire in my belly.

'Please can you dress me in the most badass thing I used to own?' I asked Hecate, looking at her. 'I'm done freaking out.'

'Boy am I glad to hear you say that,' she beamed at me, eyes flashing. 'And badass is exactly the style you want, as you're about to fight a demon.'

My fierce new resolve wobbled as I looked at her.

'A... demon?'

'Yes, but a low grade one as it's your first Trial. Trust me, they're not hard to put on their ass.'

'Hecate, the last time I fought anyone was Sam, fifteen years ago.'

'Who's Sam?'

'My brother. At least, I thought he was my brother,' I answered, sadness hitting me in the gut like a physical punch. 'I guess I won't see him again,' I whispered.

'When you're married to Hades you can do whatever the hell you like, so don't worry about it,' she said dismissively. The silver covering her ears shone as she shrugged. I opened my mouth to tell her that I would be doing whatever it took to avoid marrying Hades, but closed it again. Perhaps it wasn't such a good idea to share all my plans just yet. And if I managed to pull them off I wouldn't have to lose my brother.

'Right. So, how do I fight a demon?'

'It depends which type it is.' She turned to the wardrobe and opened it to reveal rows and rows of dresses, in every color I could imagine. 'We don't have many of your old things here, but I remember them well enough to work some magic,' she winked at me.

'Thanks,' I said. 'But seriously, how do I fight a demon?'

EIGHT

In what seemed like no time at all I was back in the throne room with Hecate, feeling slightly dizzy from the bright lurching motion of her transporting us. I managed to keep the contents of my stomach in place this time though, which I was taking as a small win.

I was wearing my white hair up in a high tail now, a silver band decorated with emerald gems keeping it back from my face. 'So as not to hinder your view of the demon', Hecate had said. My clothes too were made for 'getting out of the way', supple leather trousers that were black, and a slightly less supple leather corset that was supposed to be thick enough to repel claws. Given that the garment barely came above my breasts I wasn't sure what I was supposed to do if any claws were aimed higher.

Just stay out of the way, I told myself, as Hecate had spent the last ten minutes doing so. I was good at staying out of the way, and I was quick. This wasn't exactly what I thought I'd been training my body for when I'd hauled my ass out running every other day for the last year but I was sure glad now that I had.

The throne room was mercifully empty, and I took the opportunity to move closer to the dais. Only two thrones were on it now, massive and imposing and breathtaking. One I assumed belonged to Hades, as it looked to be made entirely from bones. I shuddered as I took in the skulls lining the arched back, the long limb bones making up the chair legs, the curved rib bones running down the raised arms. Something black that looked almost alive appeared to be holding the throne together under the bones, and I dragged my eyes from the unnerving thing to the other chair.

As fierce as the throne made from skulls was, the second throne was almost scarier. The whole thing appeared to be made of something that looked like thick barbed wire in the form of rose vines. Large metal roses with sharp, jagged edges made up the back and the seat of the chair, and I couldn't understand how anyone could ever sit on such a thing without slicing themselves to pieces. Lethal looking thorns jutted out of the tightly wound vines along the legs and arms and I shook my head with a long breath out. The two thrones were confusing and brutal to look at and they were making my nerves worse. I turned instead to the enormous flames licking up around the sides of the throne room.

'What's below us?' I asked Hecate.

'More fire,' she shrugged.

'Is there any way into this room without the magic transporty thing you do?'

'Not that I know of.'

'No, there's no other way. But if you think this is nice, you should see *my* throne room.'

I turned slowly, already knowing who had spoken. The arrogance was unmistakable.

'Zeus,' I said through gritted teeth. Hecate was bowing her head low and throwing me a pointed glare. But I wasn't going to bow my head. This was my opportunity to ensure I wouldn't be bullied by this jerk.

'You are in the presence of the Lord of the Gods. I suggest you show some deference,' he smirked. He was in the form of the blonde boy from the coffee shop.

'You owe me,' I hissed. 'You kidnapped me just to play stupid games with your brother. Until we're even you'll get no deference from me.'

I heard Hecate's intake of breath as Zeus's eyes flashed dark, and his surfer-guy build began to expand before me.

'I do believe that you need to be reminded of who I am, little mortal,' he said, his smile no longer reaching his eyes. Purple lightning began to fire around him, sizzling into the marble, but I held my ground. At this point, what did I have to lose? If I really did have to begin these Trials today, I wasn't going to start by being bullied.

I glared at him as the purple lightning flashed closer.

'Won't you be in trouble if you kill the girl you went to so much trouble to find?' I asked in a singsong voice.

'Trouble? Me? Nobody chastises Zeus!' He was three times my size now, approaching the high vaulted ceiling of the throne room, but I stayed put. My stomach was flipping and flopping as lightning screeched into the stone inches from my leather boots, but I managed to keep the flinches from showing on my face.

'Harm a single hair on her body and we'll find out once and for all which king is strongest,' hissed a voice, at the same time as my skin felt like it was being covered in ice. A smoky form shimmered into existence beside Zeus and tension literally crackled through the air. Then Zeus slowly began to shrink, the tension easing as his size decreased.

'I enjoy a woman who can stand up for herself,' Zeus said as he reached human size again. 'This might end up even more interesting than I had anticipated,' he grinned, a new, and unnerving look gleaming in his eyes. I ignored him, my gaze fixed on Hades. I wanted to see those eyes again, desperately. They had been the only thing I'd recognized here, the only thing that made some sort of sense since I'd arrived - even if I didn't know what they meant.

But all I could see were the suggestions of features, the hint of a mouth, or the tiniest flash of silver in the dark smoke. Nothing I could hold on to. He was staring back at me though, I could feel that much.

'We haven't been formally introduced,' I said, my mouth dry. 'I'm Persephone.'

There they were. For less than a second, and I almost missed it, but those silver orbs definitely flashed into existence.

'You shouldn't be here,' he said, his voice making me think of snakes.

'Yeah. I've heard. But I am, so...'

'You are human, and mortal, so you are highly unlikely to win the Trials. When they are over, you will be returned to New York.'

Relief washed through me, so strong my knees almost buckled. Hades' plan was the same as mine.

'If she survives them,' added Zeus, who was sauntering over to the thrones on the dais. A little wave of heat cut through the cold as tendrils of smoke danced out from Hades form.

'So I was right? You can't kill me? Or hurt me?' I asked Zeus, willing my confidence to build as my palms began to sweat. Sweat was my body's default reaction to any stress. Stupid body.

Zeus looked into my eyes as he waved his hands, and eleven other thrones appeared on the dais, the rose throne vanishing. He sank slowly into his own seat.

'Not during the Trials, no. And anyway, I don't want to hurt you. There are many other things I'd rather do with you...'

A stronger wave of heat blew over me, and I thought I saw Hades' chest solidify under the smoke for a second.

'Right,' I said, flexing my fingers. 'Well, in that case, I

would like to take this opportunity to inform you that you are a colossal prick.'

Hecate made a slightly strangled coughing sound and I let my smile spread fully across my face. Something fierce leapt in Zeus's eyes, but I wasn't sure it was anger.

'Oh, brother Hades. I see why you liked this one. And I can see why it was so hard to let her go.'

'Enough!' Hades shouted, and the temperature ratcheted up even higher. 'Where are the others?' he hissed, and stalked towards the thrones, his smoky legs seeming to carry more weight than should be possible. I took a few long, controlled breaths. I'd done it. I'd stood up for myself. But I wasn't sure I'd made Zeus back off. In fact I had a horrible feeling I'd just made him *more* interested in me.

'Oh, I haven't summoned them yet,' smiled the Lord of the Gods, and snapped his fingers.

The room began to morph around me, the ground rumbling and bright flashes of white light disorientating me. I was moving lower, I was sure, the ground dropping so that I was in a circular pit, stopping when I was about ten feet below the rest of the room. The dais now wrapped around the edge of the pit, the gods appearing one by one on their thrones and peering down at me. I turned slowly, seeing three new faces on the opposite side of the pit, and a man in a white toga stood next to a huge iron dish. Hecate was still standing next me in the pit and I looked at her.

'Those are the judges,' she said, without me having to ask. 'And he's the commentator. That's a flame dish, and we use them to send pictures to the rest of Olympus - like your TVs in the mortal world.'

As she spoke, gently flickering orange flames in the iron dish above us roared up, gleaming white hot, then vanished, replaced with an image of Hades' smoky form. I glanced at where the god really sat, in the throne made from skulls. A shiver took hold of me. He was staring featurelessly back at me.

'As you all now know, this is the last entrant in the Hades Trials,' he said, and I realized with a jolt that the image in the dish was speaking the same words. It was just like a camera was on him. 'There will be three rounds, each made up of three Trials. The current leader, Minthe, won five tokens. In order to beat her, Perse-phone,' his slithery voice stumbled slightly at my name and goosebumps covered my skin again, 'will need to get at least six to win. Defeat the Spartae skeleton.' He fell silent, then the commentator leapt to life, making me jump.

'Good day, Olympus! So there you have it, from the Lord of the Underworld himself. Can this last contestant beat the beloved Minthe to a spot on the Rose Throne? She's starting with an easy test, a Spartae skeleton. As you all know, the Hades Trials test the future queen in the four values that our divine gods hold most dear;

Glory, Intelligence, Loyalty and Hospitality. All things the queen of the dead will need in abundance!'

He sounded like a TV presenter from my world, and I listened intently to his over-enthusiastic words. So this was a test of glory?

'Well, I have to say, this newcomer sure looks the part, but who is she? So far we know nothing about her history or powers, but no doubt more will be revealed as we watch her fight!'

I frowned.

'If I was already married to Hades, how come they don't know who I am?' I asked Hecate quietly.

'The gods wiped you from Olympian history. Only they, and a handful of lower gods from the underworld, like me, know you ever existed.'

'Right.' Wiped from history? Didn't that seem a little extreme? *What the hell had happened?* Curiosity burned deep inside me as I tried to imagine a life in this place, but I gave myself a mental shake. I was moving on, like Athena said. All that mattered was the future.

'I have to go now. Good luck,' Hecate said, a sincere look on her beautiful, angular face.

'Thanks,' I answered her.

Her eyes turned milky white as the air around her rippled, then she was gone. A suffocating sense of how alone I was washed over me immediately. A rumbling snapped my attention to the walls of the sunken pit I was in, and I watched as patterns began to push their way out of the marble, as thought they were being carved before my eyes. The patterns were of vines, covered in grapes and leaves and twisting together as they spread across the wall until they met the place they'd started. Something about them was wrong though, and I moved closer to the stone to look. Some of the vines didn't match up properly, like two pieces of a jigsaw that didn't go together. I reached out to touch one of the areas where the vines cut off bluntly and heard a clattering sound behind me.

'Persephone will have no crowd to cheer her on today, as is the rules for the first Trial. But this is where she will win or lose supporters,' sang the commentator, excitement in his young voice. 'Will she make short work of her first demon? Or will she meet an untimely end and hand Minthe the throne today?'

I glared up at him, until the clattering got louder and dust started to gather in a large ball on the other side of the pit. My stomach tightened, my muscles tensing as the dust swirled faster, hardening into something. I shifted my weight from foot to foot, my heart beginning to hammer hard in my chest. Movement caught my eye, and I realized more carvings were appearing on the walls, but deeper, and not the same color as the stone.

Weapons. They were weapons. Twenty feet to my left was a huge sword, held up securely in the marble vines as though birthed from the wall itself. I couldn't make out what was behind the still swirling mass of dust, but there was an axe on my right, blade gleaming. I turned quickly, and saw a flail behind me in the white vines. It had a short wooden handle with a chain coming out of the end, topped with a gleaming silver ball covered in four-inch sharp spikes. I reached for it, the stone vines crumbling as soon as I touched the weapon, then reforming behind it. It wasn't as heavy as I thought it would be, but my hands still shook as I hefted it experimentally. I swung it gently as I turned back to the dust, my relief that I could use it with just one hand vanishing when I took in what was before me.

NINE

The dust had dissipated, and in its place was what I could only assume was a Spartae skeleton. It looked like it had been aptly named. The skeleton's jaw clacked open and shut unnervingly as it looked at me, and I braced my wobbling legs. It was like a Halloween outfit come to life, with gleaming white bones and empty eye sockets. And it was lifting a sword and starting to move towards me. I swung the flail in my hand, trying to build up some speed, and as though sensing the danger the skeleton immediately broke into a run. Adrenaline flooded my body, my fight and flight instincts warring with each other inside me. I held my ground, raising the flail as it whirled around, careful to keep it a good distance from my own body. Thank the gods it was so light. My pathetic attempts in the gym wouldn't have granted me the ability to wield much more.

If Hecate said this was an easy demon to defeat, then I would defeat it easily, I told myself as my breaths came shorter and the skeleton raised its sword above its head with a hiss. I swung out clumsily with the flail just before the thing got close enough to bring the sword down, aware that my weapon had a longer reach. The spike covered ball crashed into the skeleton's rib cage, bones flying and clattering to the ground as the top half of its body tipped backwards, no longer attached to the bottom. The sword fell with it, the metal ringing loudly as it hit the marble. I held my breath as the flail swung back towards me, feeling my shoulder wrench slightly as I flicked the lethal ball away. I'd done it! But... Unease trickled through my brief elation as I glanced up at the silent gods, then round at the judges. Nobody was moving, their eyes fixed on the Spartae skeleton.

Too easy. That was way, way too easy, I thought, as I looked back at the demon.

Sure enough, the scattered bones were starting to vibrate gently, then one wooshed back towards the still standing legs. I took a breath as the bones all began to zoom back, the skeleton rebuilding itself before me.

OK, I thought, fear trickling through my pumped up body. How do I defeat a skeleton that can put itself back together? I thought about every horror and fantasy book I'd ever read. Smash up the bones? Set fire to it? Freeze it? I glanced around the pit quickly, looking for anything that might be more useful. The weapon I couldn't see earlier was a crossbow, I now saw, but I didn't think that would help. The flail seemed the best bet for smashing bones. As the skeleton bent to retrieve the sword from where it lay on the floor I made my mind up. With a roar

I launched myself towards it, swinging the flail faster this time. I hurled the ball at the thing's skull, getting a kick of satisfaction as it toppled from its body with another hiss. Its bony arm reached for me and I brought the flail down through its forearm, hoping to splinter the bone, but it just severed at the joint and clattered to the floor. I moved backwards, out of the other arm's reach, then smashed my weapon down onto the bones on the floor as hard as I could. The jolt of the ball hitting the solid marble sent shockwaves through my arm and up to my shoulder, but when I lifted the ball the bones looked completely untouched.

'How-' I started, then pain blasted through my own skull and I staggered sideways as black spots appeared in front of my eyes. I felt cold bony fingers glance off my arm as I stumbled in confusion and realized foggily that I needed to move. The fucking thing had hit me, hard. My legs carried me across the small pit quickly, and I when I turned back the Spartae skeletons' skull was whizzing back into it's rightful place at the top of its long backbone.

Shit. This was going to be harder than I thought. If bone smashing wasn't an option, what else was there? I flashed on Hecate's insistence that this was supposed to be easy for someone who couldn't fight. Glory, Intelligence, Loyalty and Hospitality. Those were the things I was being tested for, according to the irritating commentator. The skeleton lifted the sword again, his jaw clacking faster than before, the sound setting my own teeth on edge. I moved slowly along the wall and he rotated to follow me. Fear began to hammer against my rational thoughts, a desperation to switch off from this crazy fucking situation growing inside me. *Come on, Persephone,* I chided myself, blinking away the dizziness. *If this is real, you have to survive. If it isn't then you've nothing to lose. Sort your shit out, now.*

Loyalty and hospitality wouldn't help me here, but intelligence... Maybe this wasn't about fighting, but about being smart. I turned quickly to the wall, and heard the demon begin to move, his bony feet clacking on the marble floor. I only had seconds.

I raked my eyes over the marble until I spotted a part of the vine pattern that didn't match up. I reached out and ran my fingers over the marble. It was warm, and when I pushed harder, I realized it was supple too. But that was all I had time to find out, and I leapt to the side just as the sword came down where I had been stood. I was faster than the skeleton was though, and I sprinted to the other side of the pit without looking back. I moved as fast as I could, scanning the walls for anywhere the vines were broken, then pulling the weird warm marble into shape, re-attaching them. As soon as the blunt ends met up the vines turned hard and cold.

I was sure I was doing the right thing, reconnecting the pattern. After all, there was nothing else in the pit, other than the demon. I was only just keeping out of its reach, having to scan the wall fast and likely missing loads, but I was making progress.

After a few laps of the room I was pretty sure I'd got all of them, and had so far avoided the blows from the demon's sword, but nothing had happened. There must be more to find, I thought, racing just ahead of the clacking footsteps as I scanned the stone desperately. My legs were beginning to tire, my breath becoming harder to catch, and my arm that still held the flail was aching.

'Aha!' I shouted in a surge of excitement as I spotted two blunt pieces of vine just a few inches off the floor. I ducked down to fix them, almost skidding as my momentum carried me fast across the marble. I knew as I dropped that I was putting myself in a seriously vulnerable position, and my heart was pounding as I tweaked the vines into place. The sword came whistling past my ear and I held my breath as I launched myself back up and away, already running, when an echoing rumble started. Without slowing I put my back to the wall, a weird side run taking over my legs until I saw that the skeleton had stilled. I slowed suspiciously, every muscle in my body humming. Had I done whatever I was supposed to? Would the demon just crumble back to dust now?

Suddenly a hole began to appear in the middle of the pit, tiny at first, then growing fast. Huge flames in many colors, the same as the ones that licked up around the side of the epic throne room, shot up through the hole as it finally stopped growing. My stomach lurched as heat washed over me. There was now a thirty-foot hole leading to a flaming abyss taking up most of the pit I was in.

Sure, I now had a way to kill the skeleton - there was no way it would survive falling into that.

But nor would I.

~

Through the flames I saw the skeleton drop its sword on the marble with a clang and I scowled. Why would it do that? Then its hollow eye sockets fixed on my face and my breath hitched. It was coming for me. I fleetingly considered trying to climb out of the pit, but the vine pattern had sunk back into the wall, the other weapons vanishing too, leaving the surface smooth. I was trapped. The skeleton was running now, close to the wall and away from the hole. It was faster without the heavy sword, I realized. Running away would be pointless as I was guessing undead skeletons didn't get tired, and I was already exhausted.

That meant it was now or never. I looked at the flail in my hand. There was no way I was giving my own weapon up.

Banking on the assumption that skeletons weren't smart, I took a deep breath and stepped closer to the flaming hole, turning my back to it and swinging the spiked ball fast. I could feel my leather clothing heat up as I got as close as I dared. Looking to my right I saw the demon closing in and I swallowed hard.

Stand your ground, Persephone. Stand your fucking ground.

The skeleton turned sharply and I sent a silent prayer of thanks to anyone listening. I'd been right, it was too stupid to be cautious. It was coming straight for me.

As the demon reached me it threw both arms out, ready to push me but I ducked and threw myself to the side, flinging the flail out towards it. The weapon connected, and I heard clattering bones as I span back around. I'd only knocked off one arm, and the bits of bone were already vibrating on the floor. I didn't hesitate, flailing the weapon back at the skeleton's head. It raised its other arm to block my blow, and the ball took the thing's wrist out. I kicked out as high as I could with my foot, my stomach lurching as I felt my leather boots connect with hard bone, but the skeleton barely budged. The fallen bones were whizzing back towards it now and panic took over. With a roar, I dropped my shoulder and barreled into its rib cage.

Mercifully, it fell. But so did I. I landed on the things chest, feeling a brief satisfaction as I felt and heard ribs give way under me, then pure terror as I rolled away and almost fell straight off the edge of the pit. A purple flame leapt up beside me and for a split second my limbs froze, fear making me unable to move. The thought of falling forever swamped my thoughts, paralyzing me. Then a voice sounded in my head out of nowhere.

You have about ten seconds before that thing puts itself back together. Move, now.

It was a male voice, and unbidden, my limbs twitched, then I was scrambling to my knees, moving away from the ledge as fast as possible. When I was a foot away I pushed myself to my feet, then turned. The skeleton's rib cage had collapsed when I'd fallen on it, its limbs scattered on the marble floor. I kicked out hard at any bit of bone I could reach with my feet, sending them flying into the flaming abyss. The demon's skull hissed as more and more bits went shooting off the edge, its detached arms flailing on the ground as I finally reached its skull. Hope shot through me as I looked down at the hollow black eye sockets. I'd won, I thought, as I gathered the last of my energy and punted the skull off the edge as hard as I could.

TEN

'Well how about that folks! Not the classiest fight we've seen, but she got the job done!' The commentator's voice boomed across the pit as the rumbling started again. The hole was closing, and the floor was rising. I threw my arms out to the side to steady myself, panting for breath as adrenaline still fizzed through me. I looked up at the gods, where Hermes and Dionysus were clapping enthusiastically, Athena and Aphrodite more slowly. The others just stared at me, Hades' smoky form flickering and Zeus's eyes gleaming.

'Now to the judges to find out what she scored!' I turned as the floor finally stopped moving, now level with the three men in grand seats. 'Radamanthus?' beamed the commentator. The man on the left, chubby and cheerful-looking, with dark bushy beard and eyebrows, smiled at me.

'One token,' he said.

'Aeacus?' The commentator asked. The second man,

skin so pale it was almost blue, spoke in a cold voice, and didn't meet my eyes.

'One token,' he said.

'And Minos?' The last man, with dark skin and a shining bald head, looked intently at me. His eyes were dark too, but bright with intelligence, and I felt like he was seeing far more of me than I was comfortable with.

'One token,' he said eventually.

'The judges are agreed! One token for Persephone. And what shall your tokens be, young lady?'

Everybody looked at me.

'What?' I stammered, and the commentator gave me a patronizing smile that made me want to punch him on the nose.

'You get to choose your tokens. What would you like to win?'

'Do I get to keep them?'

'Yes.'

'Seeds,' I said, without pause.

'Seeds?' repeated the commentator, his voice shocked and his eyebrows almost lost to his hairline. 'You want seeds?' A smile twitched on his mouth and I glared at him.

'She shall have pomegranate seeds,' said Minos, and the commentator bowed to him, hiding his smile quickly.

'Of course she shall,' he said deferentially. The air rippled in front of me, then a box appeared, floating in midair. It looked like a long ring box and when I reached for it with shaking hands, the lid popped open. Inside was a series of little chambers, and in the first,

suspended in some sort of gel, was a bright red pomegranate seed.

'Er, thanks,' I said. It wasn't quite what I'd hoped for
when I'd asked for seeds, but I hadn't expected a reward
at all, so I dropped my flail on the floor with a clatter and
closed the box. Maybe they would produce something
magnificent when I got back to New York. Something
'out of this world'. I clung to that idea as I heaved a few
deep breaths. *I'd just defeated a demon skeleton.*

'You're welcome, Persephone,' said Minos, then the
air in front of the judges rippled and they vanished.

'We'll see you for the next Trial in three days, and boy
is it a good one! Persephone will have her hospitality
tested to its limits very soon.' The commentator winked,
then he vanished too.

'Hospitality? What am I supposed to do, have
everyone over for dinner?' I said, turning back to the gods.
A wave of power rocked over me, and I dropped to one
knee without even thinking about it, bowing my head.

'Remember your place, girl,' I heard Poseidon say.

'Sorry,' I mumbled. Adrenaline and a sense of
achievement were surging through me. I'd just kicked a
demon skeleton into a multi-colored fire pit. This place
was freaking crazy, but I'd done it. I'd defeated a demon.

'Now, we must assign your guard. Then you may rest,
and prepare for the next Trial,' said Athena, and I raised
my head to look at her.

'I'd like to throw in an option, if I may?' drawled
Dionysus, and eleven heads snapped to look at him.

'Why?' asked Zeus, frowning.

'Why not?' he shrugged, a lazy smile on his face. He was wearing an open white shirt and tight black leather trousers, with huge Doc Martin boots that weren't laced up properly. The longer I looked at him, the more desperately I wanted to get steaming drunk with him.

'There are many reasons why not,' Zeus said stiffly, and turned back to me. A thought occurred to me at his words. Why wasn't Zeus putting a guard in? As if sensing my question he smiled at me.

'I don't need to assign a guard to you, dear little Persy,' he said, emphasizing the nickname he'd read on my name badge in what now seemed like a lifetime ago. 'I can come and see you myself whenever you like.'

A blast of heat pulsed out from the dais and Zeus gave Hades a sideways glance, his mouth curled in a smug sneer.

'Let's move on, please,' said Athena, and stood up. Her owl was absent now, but other than that she looked identical to when I'd met her earlier. 'There are four feathers behind you. Inspect each, then choose one.'

I turned around and sure enough, a grand desk had appeared behind me, and I could see feathers on it. I approached cautiously, setting down my seed box on the cherry-wood surface and picking up the first feather. It was almost as long as my forearm and a rich green color, with yellow edges. I ran my fingers gently down the soft edge, feeling pretty stupid. All the gods were sat behind me, watching me stroke a feather. I wished Hecate was back.

A trickle of cold suddenly tingled through my fingertips, and I got a sudden sense of grandeur and power. My brows drew together as I peered at the feather. Maybe there was more to this than I thought. I put the green feather back and picked up the next one, a fierce, solid red. Angst and irritability immediately invaded my thoughts and I put the feather back quickly. I didn't think I needed that in my life. The next feather was silver and gold, and by far the prettiest one, though the smallest. That made me instantly suspicious and I handled it carefully. When I picked it up I was surprised to feel lighter suddenly, like there was a lot less to worry about in the world. Past holidays, vacations spent relaxing and reading filled my mind. Hmmm. I was still suspicious. That seemed a little too disarming. The last feather looked like something I'd pick up in Central Park. It was a gray-brown, with a dusting of gold along the edge the only thing making it less plain. But as soon as I picked it up, a chuckle bubbled from my lips. I had no idea what I thought was funny, but the longer I held the boring feather, the more amused I felt.

'This one,' I grinned, turning to the gods. Athena closed her eyes slowly, and Dionysus did a little fist pump.

'Good choice, Persy love,' he beamed at me. His accent sounded British.

'You're an idiot,' muttered Poseidon to him, shaking his head. My eyes flicked to Hades. Was he disappointed I hadn't chosen his feather? Did it even matter? If I was stuck here in his world, surely he could see where I was all the time anyway?

'You may regret making that decision so hastily,' said Athena levelly, 'but it was a fair choice.' I put the feather back on the desk and immediately realized she was right. It had been an impulse decision because the feather had made me smile. *Shit, I should have chosen the one that felt like power.* I picked up my seed box and turned back to the gods.

'What happens now?' I asked, addressing Athena as she was still standing up.

'Now you rest. You'll meet your guard and start training for the ball tomorrow.'

'Ball?'

'Yes. Your next Trial is to host a masquerade ball. And that will conclude the first round.'

I felt my jaw drop slightly and I forced my mouth shut again. I fished desperately for something to say, but the world flashed white and I wasn't there anymore.

'I wish people would stop freaking doing that,' I snapped, as the light cleared from my eyes and I looked around the bedroom I'd been in earlier.

'Yeah, annoying isn't it,' said a now familiar voice.

'Hecate!' I whirled to see her holding two huge tumblers out and grinning like a fool.

'Told you you could do it!' she sang, and handed me one of the glasses. I took it, and on her cue we downed the contents simultaneously. If I thought whatever I drank earlier burned, then this soothed. It was like drinking honey.

'My god, that's good. What is it?'

'Gods,' corrected Hecate. 'It's Nectar.'

'As in nectar and ambrosia?'

'Yeah, except if you drank ambrosia like that it would kill you. Until you get the ichor back in your veins, at least.'

'Ichor,' I said, cocking my head at her. 'That's gods' blood, right?'

'Yup. And you're full of all that icky red human shit now,' she said, and sat down on the bed. 'Well done. I can't believe you picked seeds as your token though. You're a fucking lunatic.'

'Er, thanks?' I said, sitting beside her. 'What's wrong with seeds?'

'Well, nothing, but here you are risking life and limb, and you decide seeds are your worthy reward? Are you not worth more than that?'

'I, erm, I didn't really think about it like that. I just said the first thing I wanted. Which was seeds.'

'The other contestants all picked precious stones, emeralds and sapphires and diamonds. But you... seeds. You're an enigma, Persy.' Her bright eyes were boring into mine and I looked away uncomfortably with a shrug.

'I think I picked the wrong feather too,' I said.

'Feather? Is that how they made you choose a guard?'

. . .

It turned out that only the Trial had been broadcast via the weird iron flame dishes, so Hecate hadn't seen the feather choice afterwards, so I told her about Dionysus's feather making me laugh and my stupid impulse decision.

'Well, you could have chosen worse. Hades guard would have been strict as hell, and Poseidon's even more dull. Athena's would have been best but you could be in for something pretty entertaining from Dionysus. Just hope it's not one those randy little sprites his realm is full of.'

'Randy sprites?' I asked, slightly alarmed.

'Yeah. Did they tell you anything about the next Trial?'

'Yeah. I'll be hosting a masquerade ball,' I said, scowling. Hecate's eyebrows shot up.

'Wow, really? They've brought that one out early,' she said thoughtfully.

'Do I literally just have to plan a party?' I asked, hopefully. She gave me a look as though I were a complete idiot.

'No, Persy. You have to host a ball for some of the most disgusting and dangerous folk in Olympus. They will try to ruin the party, mostly by trying to screw or kill each other. Occasionally both. And there's always a surprise twist, something horrendous for the host to try and rectify.'

'Well, it still sounds easier than killing a skeleton.'

'It's not. Trust me.'

'Oh.'

'We'll get some specialist help in on this one. I'll send Hedone to you tomorrow.'

'Hedone? Isn't she...' I racked my memory. 'Goddess of pleasure?'

'Yup, and party planner extraordinaire. You'll love her.'

'Right,' I said.

'In the meantime, get some sleep.'

'Is this my bedroom?' I asked, looking around the room.

'Erm, yeah.'

I paused before asking, 'Was it my bedroom before?'

'No. You slept with Hades, dummy.'

'Oh.' My feelings must have shown on my face because Hecate frowned at me.

'You don't like this room?'

I shook my head, feeling guilty for complaining to her but not seeing the point in lying.

'It's just hard not having a window,' I said. She regarded me a moment, then stood up.

'I'll see what I can do tomorrow.' I gave her a grateful smile.

'Thanks.'

'You're welcome.'

'Seriously, thanks for everything,' I said, trying to impress my sincerity into the words.

'You're welcome,' she repeated.

I was asleep within seconds of my head hitting the pillow, exhaustion completely taking me over. I expected to dream about murderous skeletons or mysterious and terrifying gods made of smoke, but instead I found myself in a garden. And it wasn't a normal garden. As somebody who spent hours of their waking life dreaming up gardens, I knew instantly that this one was not born of my brain. *So whose was it?*

It was stunning, I thought, as I wandered towards an epic water feature. The word 'fountain' didn't really do the structure justice. There was a large round pool, the stone the same shining white marble from the throne room, and in its center was a statue of a man on one knee, holding a globe on his back. I recalled the ancient myth about the Titan Atlas, who was made to hold up the heavens as a punishment by Zeus. Could that be what I was looking at? As I got closer I saw that the globe was not representing my earth, but was made up of hundreds of rings, interlocking to form the sphere. Gemstones glittered in the places where the rings overlapped, and water burst from them, shining the same color as the gem until they reached the clear, sparkling pool below. I drank in the sound of the running water, the feel of the cool breeze on my face, the smell of the primroses... I turned on the spot slowly, looking at the huge array of flowers in beds lining the hedged circumference of the garden. Not all these flowers should be able to grow together. Many needed totally different temperatures and soils to the ones they were blooming right next to. I frowned.

'I heard you chose seeds,' said a voice. A male voice. Was it the voice from the Trial? The one who had told me to get up, when I'd been frozen to the spot? I realized distractedly that I hadn't told Hecate about that.

'Who are you?' I asked, quietly. It felt wrong to speak loudly in a place as serene and beautiful as this.

'I'm your friend, Persephone. I remember you well.'

'Really?'

'Of course. The Queen of the Underworld is not easily forgotten.'

'Where are you?'

'All around you. I am the garden.'

I turned on the spot again.

'Am I dreaming?'

'Of course you are. But dreams are controlled by the gods too, Persephone. I heard you chose seeds.'

'Why does everyone care so much that I chose seeds?' I said, annoyance interrupting the intense soothing effect of the garden. Another gust of wind fluttered through my hair, carrying the scent of lavender. I inhaled deeply. I wanted to stay here.

'I admire your choice. You know, pomegranate seeds can be eaten.'

I frowned.

'I'd rather plant them.'

'Trust me, my Queen. You'd rather eat them.'

I woke with a start, sitting up abruptly in the dark. Disappointment and a deep sense of loss swamped me as

I looked around at the dim bedroom, the only light coming from twinkling stars on the weird rock ceiling. It was pretty enough, but now I longed for fresh air, the scent of flowers, the sound of running water. What a weird dream. I was positive I hadn't created that garden, so whoever that voice belonged to must have. *Eat the pomegranate seed*? That was my hard-earned reward. I didn't think so. I shook my head to clear it, then lay back onto my pillows with a sigh. Everything about this place was weird. The sooner I lost the Trials and got back to New York, the better.

ELEVEN

The next time I opened my eyes the ceiling was giving off its weird daylight glow, the stars gone. What time was it? I made a mental note to ask Hecate how to keep time as I swung my legs out of bed. I was wearing a silky camisole top and matching shorts that I'd found in the wardrobe, and as weird as it was going to bed in what felt like someone else's clothes, they felt divine against my skin. I sat down at the dressing table and peered at my reflection. The make-up Hecate had put on me yesterday was gone, and my now white hair was hanging loose past my shoulders, only a slight curl left in it. But the tiny braids were still scattered throughout the bright locks. I gathered it all up into a ponytail without brushing it, and used a band on the dresser to secure it in a messy bun. My eyes still looked more green, and my cheekbones more angular. It was weird, and maybe just my imagination after defeating a demon skeleton yesterday, but I looked more fierce.

More competent. Would Ted Hammond and all those brats at school have been so cruel if I'd looked like this back then?

Probably.

There was a knock at the door and I turned my head. How did they know I was awake? I scanned the room suspiciously. *What are you expecting to find, secret cameras? In a world that uses iron fire dishes instead of TVs? Get a grip, Persy. Just roll with the punches. You'll be home in no time.*

'Yes?' I called.

'Can I come in?' came a woman's voice from the other side of the door. It was a husky, sensual voice, and I immediately felt conscious of my silky PJs.

'Erm, yeah,' I said, standing up. The door creaked open and a voluptuous woman backed in, holding two steaming mugs. My lips parted involuntarily as she turned fully to me and smiled. She had thick dark hair that looked like it would be heaven to touch, deep laughing brown eyes that gleamed with fun, and lips that looked... well nothing like any lips I'd ever seen. There was no better word for them than kissable.

'Apparently humans are into coffee in the morning,' she said, and passed me a mug with a smile. 'I'm Hedone.'

'Hi,' I stammered. 'I'm Persephone.' She nodded and sat down on the end of my bed, cupping the mug.

'Hecate is busy most of today, so she asked me to start prepping you for the masquerade ball.'

'Do you, er, help everyone out?'

She gave a tinkling laugh.

'No. But I think you're rather special, and I owe Hecate a favor.'

'Why do you think I'm special?' I asked, taking a small sip of coffee. It was utterly amazing, way better than anything we served at Easy Espresso.

'A couple reasons. I have a soft spot for humans, but more than that, I've not long taken part in some Trials of my own.' Her eyes darkened, her husky voice hardening a little. 'The Immortality Trials. They were tough, and I would like to help an underdog,' she said, looking at me.

'Underdog, huh,' I sighed, sitting down too. I wondered if Hedone was one of the few who knew I'd supposedly already been married to Hades. I didn't want to tell her if I wasn't supposed to, although it was almost impossible not to trust her. *That was her power though. Goddess of pleasure, remember?*

'Did you win your Trials?' I asked her.

'I'd rather not talk about it,' she said simply. 'Now, we have a lot to go over. Hecate said you needed some help with your clothes and make-up, then there's Olympian etiquette to cover, charm and graciousness after that, and we've all the logistics of the ball to plan. We'll need to look at the guest list, and try to anticipate what problems might be thrown your way. You'll also be having combat lessons.'

'For the ball?'

'Of course.'

'Why would I need to fight at a ball?'

'This is no ordinary ball, Persephone,' she said.

'Call me Persy,' I told her automatically. She smiled.

'This is a test to see if you are capable of holding the position of Queen of the Underworld. Politics and combat go hand-in-hand. You need to prove your ability to hold your own, support your husband and represent your realm. Social events have been at the root of almost every serious fight between the gods for centuries. They are of the utmost importance.'

'Oh,' I said. It kind of made sense that one of the Trials would be a party when she put it like that. 'That doesn't really sound like my sort of thing.'

'No? You don't like parties?'

'Or politics. I like gardens.'

Her pretty face creased into a frown.

'You're in the wrong place then,' she said. 'There aren't many gardens in Virgo.'

My heart sank as she spoke. I mean, I'd already suspected as much, but it still sucked to hear it.

'Are there any plants anywhere?'

'To be honest, I don't spend much time here, apart from with Morpheus, but I'll ask him to come and see you. He knows this place like back of his hand. Now, let's teach you how to do something better than...' she paused and looked at my hair with an awkward frown, 'well, better than that.'

'Will you show me how to do whatever Hecate did with my eyes that made them super green?' I asked her, a little over-eagerly. Hedone gave a tinkling chuckle.

'I think we may make a party-goer out of you yet,' she grinned.

We spent three full hours in the windowless bedroom, going over how to get fine black lines drawn around my eyes, creating fuller looking lips with tiny crayons, and how to get a gentle curl set into my white hair. At home I would never have allowed myself to spend so much time on such things. I mean, it wasn't like I left my apartment looking like a bag of shit, I always found time to swipe on a bit of mascara and make my cheeks a little less pale, but I'd never committed this much time to learning how to make myself look good. I'd once watched an online video tutorial for French braiding but I'd only lasted ten minutes before I wanted to throw my laptop out of the window, screaming about impossible fucking hairstyles. But Hedone made it easy to learn somehow.

'There you go,' she said, as I secured the last piece of what I now knew was called a 'crown braid' to my head. It was essentially a plait that kept my hair back from my face more stylishly and securely than my crappy bun. It reminded me of Athena's and I loved it. 'I told you you could do it.'

I beamed at her, aware that I looked like a small child receiving praise, but not really caring.

'What's next?'

'Lunch, but not with me,' she answered, tweaking my braid slightly. 'I have to go now.'

Unease at being left alone skittered through me.

'OK. Well, thanks for all your help.'

'That's OK. I'll be back this evening to go through feasting etiquette.'

'Does that mean we'll be eating a feast?' I asked hopefully.

'Yes. So go easy on lunch. See you later,' she said, and let herself out of my room, closing the door behind her.

At least she didn't do the stupid bright-light vanishing thing, I thought, looking in the mirror. What was I going to do now? I stood up and looked at the wardrobe, deciding I should probably get dressed.

Just as I was deciding between a red pantsuit type get up with a low neckline, and the green dress I'd worn yesterday, a small excitable voice sounded behind me.

'Definitely the red one.' I span around quickly, nearly dropping both outfits in surprise.

A gnome was standing on my bedroom floor, completely naked, grinning up at me.

'Who the hell are you?!'

'Skoptolis, at your service,' he bowed low, bending his three foot frame in half.

'At my service?'

'Well, technically, I'm here to guard you. I've no idea what from, but it beats what I was doing before.'

'You're my guard?' I gaped at the naked gnome. He had twinkling amber eyes, thick dark hair in a mess on top of his head with a matching beard, and massive feet. I did my best to avoid seeing if his other extremities were as large, but it was somewhat hard not to look.

'I sure am,' he said, rocking on his heels.

'Could you put some clothes on?'

'Nope.'

'Please?'

'No can do. Not allowed.'

'You're not allowed to wear clothes? Why not?'

'Dunno. Is it this that's causing the issue?' He thrust his hips forward, flicking himself at me and I spluttered as my cheeks reddened.

'Yes!'

'Ah. Does this help?' With a little pop, the gnome vanished, replaced by a dog. It was a small, terrier type dog, the same color as the gnome's hair had been, and its amber eyes still gleamed with trouble.

'Skop...' I tried to remember the name he had told me.

'Skoptolis,' said a voice inside my head. This time I did drop the clothes in surprise at hearing its voice inside my skull. 'Hello?' the voice said again, and I stared down at the dog wriggling out from under the green dress I'd just dropped on top of him. 'Is this better?' He wagged his tail.

'Yes,' I said slowly, staring at him. 'But...'

'If you want me to stay in an animal form, then I'll have to talk to you like this.'

'It's weird,' I said, frowning. 'You're in my head.'

'Then I'll go back to my normal form-' he started, but I waved my hands.

'No! No, stay like that, please.' I'd rather a wagging tail than a wagging gnome knob. 'What are you?' I asked him.

'A kobaloi.'

'Are you, by any chance, a randy sprite?'

'*I have my moments,*' he answered, tail wagging faster as he leapt up onto the bed beside me. I automatically reached out to stroke his fur, then paused. Was that weird? He's not actually a dog, he's a naked, hairy gnome, I reminded myself. '*If you put that red thing on, you'll find out just how randy I can be.*' I snatched my hand back.

'Then I'll go with the green,' I muttered, scooping the clothes up off the floor as I stood up. I strode to the washroom with the green dress, and heard Skoptolis jump to the floor behind me. 'Erm, where are you going?' I said, turning to him.

'*I have to guard you.*'

'In my own bathroom?'

'*Yup.*'

'No way.' The dog wagged its tail faster as I glared into his eyes.

'*But you've seen all my bits and bobs,*' he protested, his mental voice still light and laughing, like that damned feather I'd chosen.

'I don't care, you're not seeing mine!' I exclaimed.

'*Please? I bet they're really nice.*'

I rolled my eyes.

'Not a fucking chance,' I said sternly. 'Now wait here, you pervert.'

'*You can call me Skop,*' he said, tail still wagging furiously.

'Whatever,' I grumbled and slammed the door shut behind me.

I stepped back out of my washroom in the green dress a few minutes later, and jumped when I saw Hecate sitting on the edge of my bed and scowling at Skop, who was back in naked gnome form.

'Dionysus is a jerk,' she said, looking up at me.

'Let me guess,' I grinned. 'Don't tell him you said that.'

'Exactly,' she answered, with another grimace at Skop.

'I thought we'd agreed on something furry,' I said to him.

'I can make this furry if you want,' he beamed, reaching down.

'Put that the fuck away!' snapped Hecate, and the kobaloi gave an infectious giggle, before shifting back into dog form. 'What was that drunken idiot thinking, sending you a kobaloi as a guard?' she said, shaking her head.

'*He was thinking that you were far more likely to need cheering up than guarding,*' Skop said in my head, and I couldn't help but warm to him, and Dionysus, a little.

'Who knows,' I shrugged. 'I still don't know why I need a guard at all.'

'Me either. Anyway, I have good news.' I quirked an eyebrow at her as she clapped her hands together. 'I have convinced Hades to give you a new room. A new room, above ground.'

Gratitude hit me all in a rush and I flung my arms around Hecate without thinking. She gave an awkward squeak. 'There's a catch!' I let go and narrowed my eyes at her. 'It's not normal for contestants to be given the finest rooms in the Underworld. So you're going to need to earn it. Publicly. To avoid awkward questions.'

'Right,' I said, slowly.

'There will be another Trial. This evening. If you win, you can have the new room.'

'OK. Sounds fair,' I said, anxiety and anticipation skittering through me.

'Also, you have to have lunch with Hades.' She spoke so fast I almost didn't catch her words.

'What?' My stomach twisted as I gaped at her. 'When?'

'Now. Have fun!' she said, and the world flashed white once more.

TWELVE

'Damn Hecate,' I hissed, as I gazed around at the room I was in, heart racing as I tried to take it in. It reminded me of a church, massive vaulted ceilings stretching above me, all made from white marble. Intricate weaving patterns ran down the stone everywhere, depicting vines and plants and flowers, butterflies flitting amongst everything. Huge drapes, at least twenty feet tall, lined the two longest sides of the room. In the center was a large table laid for two, next to a circular raised platform. The platform was empty and something about it seemed wrong. Really wrong.

I stepped closer to it, frowning as a hollow feeling spread through my gut, something akin to grief pulling at me. Why would an empty platform make me feel such a sense of loss? Giving up on trying to work out the unsettling feeling, I turned to the table. There was nothing remarkable about it, except that it was a little large for two and dressed beautifully. There was, however, something remarkable about the two chairs drawn up to it. Just like the grand thrones I had seen in the fiery throne room, these were decorated with skulls and roses. But where the thrones were bold and intimidating, these were elegant and stunning. And even more interestingly, they both had skulls *and* roses carved into the rich mahogany wood. The vines of the roses twisted around the skulls seamlessly on both chairs, and something about the pattern felt oddly satisfying. The two elements were drawn together perfectly, displaying the angry skulls and the fierce roses as equally dangerous and beautiful. They were nothing like the angry thrones.

As I reached out to touch the wood of the closest chair, a voice spoke sharply behind me.

'How did you get in here?'

I whirled around, starting at the words, then feeling a violent shiver rock though me as I saw the smoky form of Hades.

'Hecate sent me here. With the white-light-flashy thing you all do,' I said too quickly, trying to swallow the fear that leapt up inside me. 'I assumed you were expecting me.'

He let out a sigh, the smoke rippling around him.

'That woman needs to learn to meddle less.'

'Oh. Should I go?' I asked hopefully. The smoke rippled, and I caught the briefest flash of silver eyes.

'You shouldn't be here at all.'

'I didn't ask to be,' I snapped, unable to help myself. 'Why would I want to be in a place with no outside?' The smoky form rippled again.

'The Underworld is no place for you.' His voice was cold and harsh.

'Then send me home,' I said, my palms suddenly sweating at the thought that he could actually send me back. *Please, please send me home.*

'I can't,' he hissed, and the temperature suddenly shot up. 'My bully of a brother has spoken.' At the word bully, my fear receded slightly, and I cocked my head. Hades felt bullied? That couldn't be right. How could a king be bullied?

'Why don't you stand up to him?' I asked, the brazen words almost failing me as I spoke them. The temperature soared again as smoke billowed from him.

'You think I haven't tried that?' he said loudly, and images of fire began to lick at my mind, the iron tang of blood creeping onto my tongue.

'Please, please don't!' I begged, hearing and hating the fear in my voice, but not able to hide it. 'Not again.'

The fear lessened immediately, the images vanishing as the room cooled.

'This is no place for humans,' Hades snapped. 'You are likely to get yourself killed here.'

'You mean you're likely to scare me to death!' I snapped back, my nerves frayed. 'How the hell am I supposed to have lunch with you if you frighten the shit out of me every time I ask you something you don't like?'

The smoke rippled.

'Lunch?'

'That's what Hecate said.' My head was starting to

pound. I'd only met the man twice and I already hated being around him.

'That infernal woman,' Hades muttered. There was a long silence, then he spoke. 'Are you hungry?'

'No,' I lied. 'You can just send me back to my room.' He paused before answering.

'I'm told you don't like your new room.'

New room? Hecate's word flicked into my head. '*You used to share a room with Hades, dummy.*' How? How had I ever shared a room with that thing? Even if you took the fact that he was made of smoke out of the equation, as far as I could tell he had no personality whatsoever, let alone a sense of humor. Plus he was terrifying. I prayed he wouldn't mention the fact that we were supposedly married once.

'It's very nice, but there aren't any windows. I spend most of my time outside, back at home,' I said, as politely as I could manage.

'There is an outside here,' he said curtly, and I noticed the hissing sound had lessened in his voice.

'Really?' He raised a smoky hand, and the drapes along each side of the room withdrew slowly, and my breath caught in my throat. *Sunlight.* I hurried to the glass windows that had been hidden behind the fabric, and recoiled slightly. The land beyond was completely barren. Cracked, dry earth stretched for miles, and other than a few bare stubborn trees, nothing lived.

'What happened?' I breathed.

'Nothing will grow,' he said bluntly. 'But I believe it still counts as 'outside'. What is that?' I turned to him as he asked the question, and saw his smoky arm pointing towards my feet. I looked down and blinked as I saw Skop, sitting still and blinking back up at me.

'That's my new guard.'

'It's a kobaloi. Why would you need a kobaloi as a guard? All they do is play tricks on people and try to screw everything,' he said. Skop's tail wagged and a smile sprang unbidden to my lips.

'Apparently Dionysus was under the impression that I needed entertainment more than guarding,' I said.

'He was wrong.' I took a deep breath. Hades thought I needed a guard too? Some of the iciness had left his voice, and the addition of the, albeit faint, sunlight to the room was helping to ease my racing pulse. I gathered my courage, deciding to try to get whatever information I could out of the man I was supposed to have once liked enough to marry.

'Will you tell me why I need a guard?'

'No.'

'Am I in danger, or is Poseidon right, am I the one who's dangerous?' I pushed.

'Neither.'

I decided to change tack. Hades hadn't scared me for a full three minutes now, and I was feeling bolder the longer we spoke.

'Why does the temperature change when you're angry? Why is it cold sometimes and hot others?'

'That's enough questions.'

'No it's not! I know nothing about this world, surely I deserve a few harmless questions answered?'

'Deserve?' He rippled.

'Yes, *deserve*. Do I need to remind you that I've been abducted to the freaking Underworld and made to fight demons for a life I don't understand?'

The smoke form contracted quickly, almost turning solid but not quite. There was long silence, and my heart began to hammer again. Had I gone too far?

'It only gets hot when I haven't got control of my temper,' Hades said suddenly, and I was sure the hissing sound had gone from his voice completely. 'If I'm scaring on purpose, it's cold.'

My eyes snapped to where I knew his were. *He was answering me.*

'Are you made of smoke deliberately?' I asked, quickly, as though I needed to get all my questions in before he changed his mind.

'Yes.'

'Why?'

'I don't want people to know what I look like.'

'Why not?'

'I'm the Lord of the Dead.'

'That's not an answer,' I said, cocking my head at him and scowling.

'Yes, it is.'

'No, it's not. Are you trying to be more scary?'

'No. I'm trying to-' he cut off abruptly. 'I don't need to tell you this,' he said. His voice was definitely different now, deep and rich where it had been cold and scratchy. I took a long breath, and went for the question I most wanted to ask him, almost hoping he would say no.

'Can I see your eyes?'

'No,' he said, but the word was soft.

'Please?' I stepped towards him, staring into his smoky, featureless face.

'Why do you want to see them?' he asked.

'Because... When I saw them yesterday, I knew I wasn't dreaming. I knew this was real,' I said, knowing I was telling him too much, but not able to stop myself. 'They're the only thing I recognize in this world.'

Hades' form flashed, and suddenly, there they were. Those intense, beautiful silver eyes. But they were filled with sadness, and pain so evident that my breath caught.

In an under a second they were gone again, and I let out my breath slowly. The desire to help him, to make him happy, to fix whatever made him so intensely sad was overwhelming me. I scrabbled for something to say but Hades spoke first.

'You must leave. I'll tell Hecate not to plan something so stupid again,' he said, the hiss back in his voice. Coldness washed over my skin, and I didn't know if it was his power or my own emotions.

'But-' I started, but he cut me off, his voice making me think of snakes when I didn't want to. I wanted to hold onto that emotion, that feeling of intensity. *I wanted to help him.* 'Do not talk to me again. You will not be here much longer.'

Anger cut through my confusion, as my feelings were doused out instantly. One minute he was making me feel all this overwhelming emotional crap, the next he was being a dick to me?

'I hope not,' I snapped.

'Lose the Trials, then leave my realm,' he said, his tone hard and arrogant and cold. Something ragged and desperate gnawed at my gut, but my conflicting feelings were resolving themselves as anger.

'With pleasure,' I spat, glaring at him.

THIRTEEN

'**W**ell, that was rude,' said Skop as I threw myself down on my bed.

'I wish they'd stop flashing me about all over the fucking place,' I fumed. 'Why can't they just use doors and stairs like normal fucking people?'

'*I like it when you swear,*' Skop said as he jumped up beside me. '*Feisty women are just my type.*'

'Not now, Skop. I am seriously not in the mood. I thought you were here to cheer me up.'

'*I am. Would you like me to take a shit in one of his shoes?*'

A bark of laughter escaped my lips.

'Very much, but I'm not even sure he wears shoes. He's made of smoke.'

'*Nah, he's got clothes on under there.*' I raised my eyebrows at the dog.

'You can see through his smoke?'

'*Yeah.*'

'What does he look like?' I hated myself for asking, but I was incredibly curious.

'I'm mostly into women, but he's pretty tasty.'

'Right,' I said, rolling my eyes.

'You'll see him soon enough,' Skop said, trotting about in a little circle on the covers, then settling down in a tight ball.

'I doubt that. He just told me never to talk to him again.'

'Which is angry-man-god-speak for: I'd very much like to have sex with you.'

'Don't be ridiculous,' I said, but a frisson of something skittered through my core at his words. *Smoke. He's made of smoke, fills your head with dead people and has just demonstrated that he's a total dick. Do not go there.*

Hades was definitely one bad boy too far.

I spent the next half an hour trying to learn how to talk to Skop in my head, like he did to me. I had to project the words I was thinking to him, which was harder than it sounded. After a while though, I started to get the hang of it.

'Will I be able to talk to everyone like this?' I asked him silently.

'Nope, only sprites, magical objects you've bonded with, or powerful beings.'

'What about Hecate?'

'I dunno, you'll have to ask her.'

As if on cue, there was a knock at the door and it swung open before I could answer.

'Speak of the devil,' I muttered, as Hecate strode into the room, a large tray laden with sandwiches in her arms.

'I am so, so sorry,' she said, then frowned. 'The devil? Isn't that what you call Hades in your world?'

I gulped.

'Yes. And you sent me for lunch with him without even telling him!'

'I know, I know, I thought it was a good idea for you two to catch up!'

'Well, it wasn't.'

'Tell me about it. I've just had my ass handed to me. I'm surprised I didn't get demoted,' she said, blowing out a sigh and setting the tray down. 'You look smoking hot by the way. Love your hair like that.'

Once I'd forgiven Hecate for her misguided attempts at my marital reconciliation, I got changed into leather fighting garb and she took me to where I would be learning combat. Mercifully, we did use stairs and doors to reach the training hall, the maze of blue-torch-lit tunnels rendering me lost in a matter of minutes.

'Can you remember how to get back if I ever get lost?' I silently asked Skop, trotting along at my side.

'*Course I can,*' he told me cheerfully.

The training hall was a large cavern, with the same daylight glowing ceiling as my room had, and a distinctly Greek vibe about it. Columns lined the walls, and the space behind them was filled with open crates. Hecate made her way straight to one in particular and began to rummage about.

'Did you bring the dagger I gave you?'

'Course,' I said, pulling it from the little sheath that was attached to my belt. The fighting clothes had straps and pouches and loops for weapons all over them.

'Good. Put it down over there and don't come anywhere near me with it.'

'OK,' I said, and laid it on the floor. Skop sniffed it, then trotted away quickly.

'Here,' Hecate said, straightening and holding out a similarly sized dagger. I went to her, taking it and peering into the other boxes. They were filled with weapons. 'The floor will absorb shock when you land on it, so you won't hurt yourself,' she said.

'When I land on it?'

'Yup,' she said, then out of nowhere kicked her leg out towards me. She managed to swipe both my ankles at the same time, and I yelped as I crashed to the floor, the dagger skittering away from me. She was right about the floor - it morphed beneath me into something spongy as soon as I landed, but my ass still hurt as I hit. 'Lesson number one: when you're in this room or any fighting pit, you need to be constantly vigilant.' I glared at her.

'You think you could have told me that before we came in here?'

She grinned at me.

'Lesson number two: nothing is fair.'

'Lesson number three: your teacher is an asshole,' said Skop in my head, and I suppressed a smirk.

Hecate spent the next hour teaching me how to use a dagger in close combat. It mostly involved hiding what your intentions were, or finding gaps to get the thing through, and in no time at all I was frustrated and tiring.

'I need to get back to running,' I panted, as Hecate whirled easily out of my grasp for the fifth time.

'Running? Being fast will only get you so far. We need to build up your tolerance, teach you how to take a few hits,' she said, dancing on the balls of her feet, her fists raised.

'Am I the only human in the Trials?' I asked her, mostly just to lengthen the pause and get some energy back.

'Yup.'

'What about the current winner, what's she?'

'A mountain nymph. She has earth powers.'

'Huh. So living underground's not a problem for her, I guess.' I thought about what I'd learned about my own supposed powers in the throne room. 'And my powers were to grow plants?'

'Kind of, yeah.'

'Kind of?'

'Stop asking questions, Persy,' she said, and danced towards me. I lifted my arms quickly into a defensive position, flicking my dagger out towards her.

It seemed my short break was over.

～

Eventually Hecate announced we'd done enough, and I should save my energy for that evening's Trial. I didn't know what energy she was referring to, I was wiped out. But when we returned to my room, Hecate produced some of the wine she'd given me when I'd first arrived.

'This will revitalize you,' she grinned, and poured us both glasses. 'We have an hour until the Trial.'

I drank some of the wine, immediately feeling more alive, more alert. Weird. Wine in my world dulled the senses.

After a while, we began to talk about what to expect in my next Trial. Hecate thought it was unlikely that I would be fighting again, so soon after the last fighting Trial, and it wasn't likely to be a hospitality test either, as that would be covered by the masquerade ball.

'So it's going to be intelligence or loyalty,' she mused. 'Or glory in a different way from fighting.'

'How do they test loyalty?' I asked. She looked sideways at me, an uneasy expression taking over her face.

'To be honest with you, Persy, that's usually the worst Trial. It'll be something you won't expect, and you won't always be told the world is watching.'

'So they'll try and trick me?'

'Yes.'

'And I won't even know I'm in a Trial?'

'Not necessarily. If there's no chance of you beating Minthe, they might let you off lightly.'

'Is Zeus designing all the Trials?' I asked, taking another sip of fortifying wine.

'No, all the Olympians are involved.'

'Do they get on with each other?'

Hecate snorted. 'Absolutely not.'

'What did Hades do to upset Zeus?' I asked the question casually, although I was burning to know the answer.

'He broke one of their very few sacred rules. He created new life in Olympus.'

'Life? But he's all about the dead.' I frowned at Hecate, and she cocked her head at me.

'Hades isn't like the other Olympians, Persy. There's far more to him than people see.'

I thought about those silver eyes, so full of emotion. But then the fire, the taste of blood, the smell of burning filled my head and I sighed.

'People only see smoke,' I said.

'He wasn't always like that,' she answered quietly. Something in my stomach tightened.

'What happened?' I asked, but deep in my gut, I already knew the answer.

'You.'

FOURTEEN

I t seemed like no time at all until I was standing in front of the gods again, lined up on their thrones, building-sized flames dancing on either side of the floating throne room. I found my eyes fixed on Hades' smoky form, framed by the intimidating skulls making up the back of his huge seat. My palms began to sweat.

'Good day, Olympus!' the commentator's voice rang out suddenly, and I whirled to see him stood behind me.

'Gods, he's irritating,' said Skop's voice in my head, and I glanced down at him, sat by my feet.

'Agreed,' I told him silently.

'So today we have an unannounced Trial! As our little Persephone is human, and as such the only contender with no powers, she will be granted an additional reward if she completes this test.'

I pictured a room with windows, the idea of not being underground hardening my resolve. *Even if the view was of a barren wasteland.*

'He wasn't always like this.' Hecate's words replayed in my head. She had refused to say anymore, and my frustration at the tidbits of my past she was dropping was getting harder to suppress. Had I caused that wasteland outside too? What had I done?

'The Trial will be one of Glory,' beamed the commentator, and my pulse quickened. *Please not fighting, please no demons,* I prayed. 'Today we get to see Persephone face some of her fears,' he sang, and I felt my stomach lurch. My fears? How would they know what my fears were? If there was a single fucking spider involved, the room with windows would have to go, I thought, as anxiety ratcheted my temperature up. 'We will not be performing the Trial in the throne room though, so let us away to the chasm!'

'What?' I started to say, but that damn white light flashed again and everything was gone.

When the light cleared from my eyes, I swear my heart stopped beating for a moment. I was standing on the edge of a sheer drop. I stumbled backwards, my heart in my throat, as my knees began to wobble. I instinctively crouched down, to lower my center of gravity and to stop myself falling if my legs did actually give out. My head swam as vertigo began to swamp my working senses, nausea building as I stared over the edge of the drop. Whoever had spoken to me during the last trial had known I was too scared to move when I was flung to the edge of the hole in the fighting pit. They'd known I was terrified of heights. Was this their doing?

Get a grip. Get a grip. You're nowhere near the edge. You don't even know what you have to do yet. I forced myself to look around, taking deep breaths. I would be better once the adrenaline kicked in, and surged me past the initial fear.

I was outside. Actually outside, after days of wanting to be. There was nothing but dull beige sky above me, and the cliff edge I was crouching on was gouged out of the dry, dusty ground. There was another cliff opposite me, forming the other side of what I assumed the commentator had been referring to as the 'chasm' and all of the gods were there, lined up on their thrones, their faces too distant for me to make out expressions. I took more deep breaths, trying to feel a breeze or take comfort from the fact that I was no longer underground, but it felt no different. The air didn't move, the temperature was neither cool nor warm, there were no scents filling my nostrils. It didn't feel like any outside I was used to.

'Hecate? Skop?' I called hopefully.

'I'm on the other side,' said Skop in my head, and I was surprised by how much comfort I drew from hearing his voice.

'I'm scared of heights,' I said too quickly, as though expressing my fear might expel it. It didn't.

There was a long pause.

'Shit,' he said eventually.

.   .   .

'So here we are at the chasm! As you all know from previous contestant's Trials, this is a particularly nasty part of the underworld,' rang out the commentator's voice. 'Fall down there and you'll fall forever.' Bile rose in my throat. *Fall forever?* Being burned up by magic flames was one thing, but to fall forever? Goosebumps rose on my skin. I genuinely couldn't think of many things more terrifying. 'All Persephone needs to do to complete the Trial is get to the other side. Good luck!'

'What?' I exclaimed aloud. How the fuck was I supposed to get to the other side? There were no bridges, and the chasm was at least twenty meters across so jumping wasn't an option. Not that I'd have been able to jump over a freaking one meter gap, if it was over an endless void. 'How?' I yelled. I stared over at the gods, small in the distance. Nothing. I turned on the spot, staying crouched to stop my legs from shaking. The three judges were a few meters behind me, sitting on their grand seats and surrounded by empty, cracked land. 'Oh!' I said in surprise. None of them responded, their gazes boring into mine. I couldn't see anything else, so I turned back to the chasm. Maybe there was a bridge further down. But to find out, I would have to move closer to the edge.

I sat down, my insides shaking. For years and years I hadn't even been able to climb a step-ladder. It didn't matter how resolute or rational I was in my thoughts, my body betrayed my mind every time I was in a position where I could potentially fall. My legs and hands would shake, my breathing would become too shallow, and my vision would start to blur as dizziness took over.

You know what's coming, I told myself. *So you can deal with it. You can do this.*

I shuffled forwards on my butt, closer to the edge. I was only a foot away, so I didn't have to move far before my feet reached the precipice. I drew my knees up, and shuffled farther forward, forcing myself to take deep, slow breaths. I could see the chasm clearly now, and I looked left to right, trying to spot a bridge. There was nothing.

'It's invisible,' said Skop's voice in my head.

'What?'

'*You're sort of at a disadvantage here, as you're not from Olympus and have no power, so I feel it's only fair I tell you. The bridge is invisible.*'

'Then how the fuck am I supposed to cross it?' I hissed back in my mind.

'*You have to feel for it. Then hope you walk straight. Or go across on your butt. That works too.*'

'Feel for it? Are you fucking psychotic?' If my heart beat any faster I was sure I'd throw up. Or have a heart attack and drop down dead. Although I'd rather that than cross an invisible bridge over an endless fall. 'There is no fucking way I'm doing this.'

'*Try.*'

I started at the voice, my breath catching. *It wasn't Skop's.* It was the same one I'd heard in the last Trial.

'Who are you?' I yelled. I had no way of answering

him in my head, as I couldn't project my thoughts at someone totally unknown.

'Reach forward, and feel for the bridge.'

'No! Did you tell them I was scared of heights?' My voice trembled.

'It's a foot to your left,' the voice continued, ignoring me.

My whole body was covered in sweat now, my back slick under the leather corset. I shuffled a foot to my left, my damp hands shaking as I put them flat on the ground and lifted myself sideways. Dust stuck to them as I drew them back around my knees.

'Good. Now, reach forward.'

I closed my eyes, but it did nothing to lessen the rising panic. *Come on, come on, come on. They're not going to let you die this early in the competition. Get a grip.* I shuffled backwards a little, then swiveled onto my belly, wishing I could hear anything other than my heart hammering against my ribs to distract me.

'This place sucks,' I hissed aloud, as I gripped the edge of the cliff with my sweaty hands. My head was too far back to see over the edge, which was exactly how I needed it to be. 'And I bet I look like a fucking idiot.' Memories flashed into my mind of me being sprawled on my front on the ground before, each time because some jerk had tripped me or pushed me, to make everyone else laugh. The thought sent a spurt of determination through me, and I moved my fingertips along the edge carefully. Then my right hand hit something hard. Slowly, I began to feel around, wriggling my way closer, but keeping an arm's length from the precipice. Skop had been right. There was a bridge. It was cool and smooth to touch, like plastic or metal and I could grip each edge with my hands. It couldn't be more than two feet wide. Very, very slowly, I drew myself up onto my elbows and knees, still gripping the edges of the bridge so I didn't lose it, and keeping my eyes squeezed shut. The muscles in my thighs were vibrating, and another wave of dizziness crashed over me as I inhaled deeply. *You've worked yourself up into this mess of nerves,* I scolded myself. *Just get on with it. You're holding the edges of the bridge, you won't fall off. Just crawl across. Olympus is watching.*

I moved one knee forward, my stomach lurching as I did so. My survival instincts were begging me to open my eyes, but common sense and fear kept them closed. It was an *invisible* bridge. There was no way I wanted to look down as I did this. I slid one shaking hand along the edge of the bridge, my skin slick against the material. I pushed gently, testing my weight. It felt solid. I let out a long breath, then repeated the movement on my other side. Knee forward, hand forward. Again. And again. *I could do this.*

And I probably could have, if my traitorous eyes hadn't flickered open.

Black dots instantly invaded my vision as the image before me swam and warped. Icy cold fear clamped onto my muscles as I stared down into black nothingness, the sides of the rocky chasm stretching on endlessly beneath me. Fresh nausea swamped my insides and I couldn't think straight. *Get off the bridge, get off the bridge, get off the bridge.* Over and over the words sang through my head, drowning out anything else. I felt my right leg spasm and jerk, and pure terror bit into me as my right hip collapsed. I had no idea how far across the bridge I'd got, blind panic obliterating facts as my body began to shut down. Pain lanced through my head as I crumpled onto the bridge and my chin banged into the hard material. I barely registered the taste of blood as I flung my arms around the bridge, squeezing my eyes closed again as they filled with tears of fright.

'Persephone! Go back the way you came, you're not far!' Skop's alarmed voice rang in my mind and I focused on his words. *You're not far.* I forced my shaking, numb legs back up, not caring one jot how I must look with my front half wrapped around an invisible bridge, shoving my butt in the air. *'That's it, you're doing great.'* I began to shuffle backwards, one painstaking inch at a time, my hands shaking so badly I could barely use them. *'You're almost there, your legs are off the bridge now,'* Skop said, his voice strained but clear.

When my hands hit a solid barrier, I knew I'd reached the cliff. Painstakingly slowly, I unwrapped the fingers of my left hand from the bridge, then did the same with the other. Tears were streaming down my cheeks as I held my breath, straightened and opened my eyes. *I was off the bridge.* I scrambled backwards, far away from the edge, and looked across at the gods through tear-blurred vision. None of them moved.

'I can't do it!' I yelled, my whole body vibrating. I felt sick. *My stupid, stupid fucking body and my stupid,*

stupid fucking brain won't let me do it. A sob escaped me and I swore viciously. I hadn't wanted to look weak. I hadn't wanted to make myself a target. I was supposed to be the underdog who would hold her own.

But look at me. Sobbing and shaking like a little girl, too frightened to cross a damned bridge.

And the whole of Olympus had seen me fail.

FIFTEEN

'This room isn't that bad,' said Skop as he jumped up onto the bed beside me. I pulled the covers further over my head.

'It's not about the fucking room,' I snapped. And honestly, knowing that the view out of the window that I hadn't managed to win would be that awful wasteland, I meant it. 'It's about looking like a fucking idiot in front of the whole damn world.'

'Maybe nobody was watching today,' the kobaloi said.

'Yeah, right.' Zeus, Athena, Hades, all of the gods were watching. They'd all seen me go to pieces, fail spectacularly at a test of glory. They'd all seen the judges award me zero tokens, before I was flashed back to my bedroom, shaking and crying. I screwed my face up and shouted abuse into my pillow. I was so angry with myself. I felt like my body had betrayed me, and I couldn't do anything about it. The feeling of impotence, the lack of anyone else to blame, the memories of spending years feeling too weak to achieve anything were overwhelming me. Fury was starting to build deep down in the pit of my stomach, and I had no outlet. I couldn't hide in this bed forever. But how the hell could I show my face?

I knew very little about this world, and I had no idea just how many people had witnessed my breakdown. But even one person seeing it was one too many. My fears were exposed, and I was a failure.

'Have you always been afraid of heights?' asked Skop, his voice gentler than usual.

'Yes.'

'Do you have any other fears?'

'None so fucking debilitating,' I spat. Shame was burning inside me, fueled with anger. I wanted to escape my own body, be somebody else. Anybody else.

'Good. They can't use the same test twice. So that's the worst out of the way.'

I peeked over the edge of the comforter and looked at him.

'Really? I'll never have to do that again?'

'Nope.'

'Thank fuck for that.' A little slither of relief, or hope, cut through the shame. But I still had to go out there again. I still had to show my face, after looking so utterly pathetic.

There was a loud knock at my door, and I drew the comforter back over my head.

'Go away!' I shouted.

'You know, hiding under the covers is not really

helping your image,' said Hecate, and I heard the door shut behind her. Shame shivered through me again.

'What am I supposed to do, just pretend it never happened?'

'Yes. That's exactly what you need to do. Shrug it off like you couldn't give a shit.'

'How?' I pulled the covers down and looked at her. There was no pity in her beautiful face as she stood over my bed, hands on her leather-clad hips.

'Everyone has weaknesses. The whole point of these Trials is to expose them. You're lucky. Yours is out of the way early. You need to stand in front of the world and act like it's totally fucking normal to not be able to cross an invisible bridge over an endless chasm, and make everyone believe you're going to ace all the other tests.'

I stared at her, playing her words back. Part of me knew she was right. People were not superheroes. And nobody was fearless. *But everyone else has powers. You're the underdog, the weakling,* the other, shitty part of my brain pointed out.

'I've reminded everybody that I'm human, and inferior,' I said quietly.

'I don't mean to sound like a bitch, but they already knew that. They didn't need reminding. Nobody out there expects you to win anything at all.'

'Then why the hell am I here?' I exploded. 'Just to be made a mockery of?'

Hecate threw her arms in the air, giving me an exasperated look.

'Yes! You already know that! Zeus brought you here

to piss off Hades! It wasn't anything to do with you personally!'

I let out a cry of frustration.

'Nothing to do with me *personally*?! This is bullshit! This is completely unfair and I've had enough.' I kicked the covers off viciously, and leapt to my feet. 'Where's Zeus?'

A surprised expression crossed Hecate's face, then a smile began to form on her lips.

'Persy, I'm glad to see you angry instead of wallowing in shame, but I don't think having it out with the lord of the gods, most powerful being in Olympus, is a very good idea.'

'He can't hurt me until after the Trials. I want to talk to him.' Fury was rolling through me now, fire burning in my belly.

'No,' she said flatly. I snarled and she raised her eyebrows. 'You can fight me instead. In the training room.'

I glared at her, but the more I thought about it, the more I wanted to train with her. I wanted to kick and punch and scream and shout.

'Fine. What kind of sadistic asshat designs an invisible bridge, anyway?' I hissed eventually.

'*My thoughts exactly,*' agreed Skop in my head.

The more blows I landed on Hecate, and the more I felt my skin bruising and my muscles aching, the less useless I felt. I was made of flesh and blood, and pounding my fists into training pads reminded me of that fact. Seeing the material dent when I landed a kick squarely in the center, seeing the wooden staffs strain when I smashed them into Hecate's weapon - it proved that I *did* have an impact.

'This is much, much better than this morning,' panted Hecate. 'And now I'm starving. It's late.'

We ate together in my room. We didn't talk much, too intent on devouring a meal of roast chicken and carrots.

'Did any of the other contenders fail at a Trial?' I asked as I swallowed my last mouthful.

'Yeah, loads. There's usually nine Trials, in three rounds, and Minthe only got five tokens and is in first place.'

'Usually nine?' I asked. Relief that I wasn't the first to fail mingled with curiosity. 'Is there a chance that I'll do less than nine?'

'Um, yeah. A couple girls did less,' she said evasively.

'There's only one way that'll happen,' said Skop. I threw him a bit of chicken and he leapt to his feet, tail wagging.

'Skop, don't tell her!' said Hecate.

'I swear to god, if I hear the words "don't tell her" one more time-' I started, but Hecate cut me off.

'Gods!' she said loudly, sighing. 'I'll keep correcting you until you get it right. It's *gods*, not god.'

'Whatever! Why did those girls do fewer Trials?'

Hecate dropped her eyes to her empty plate.

'They died.'

I blinked.

'Died? In... in the Trials?'

'Yeah.' I set my plate down beside me and Hecate

stood up, grabbing it quickly. 'Right, well, I'd better be off to bed. Hedone is back tomorrow, helping with the ball preparations.'

'They let people die?' I said, staring at her.

'They're not allowed to intervene, Persy.'

I opened my mouth to argue that somebody kept talking to me during my Trials, but closed it again. So far, it seemed the owner of the voice was trying to help me, and if that was against the rules, I should probably keep quiet about it.

'I knew this was dangerous but...'

'Keep training like you did just now, and do what Hedone tells you and you'll be fine.'

My rational voice spoke in the back of my head. *None of this is real anyway, who gives a shit if you die in this made-up place?*

But I didn't believe the voice anymore. I couldn't, no matter how much I wanted to. I knew it was nothing but a last-ditch attempt by my rational conscious to explain the insane circumstances I'd found myself in.

But as insane as they were, I knew in my heart they were real.

I didn't think I'd been asleep long when I stepped into the beautiful, ethereal garden again. The tinkling sound of water was interrupted by the chirruping of birds, and I looked up, scanning the trees.

'You won't see them. There's much you won't see until you fully accept this world.'

The voice was deep and calm, just like before.

'Is it you who keeps talking to me during the Trials?' I asked, walking towards the Atlas fountain.

'I can only talk to you in your sleep, dear girl,' he answered. I stopped, crouching down by a patch of flowers and running my fingertips gently over the petals. A shiver of satisfaction rippled through me. This place was perfect. 'You are afraid of heights?'

The question tainted the serene feeling I was enjoying and I scowled.

'A fact you and the rest of Olympus are now aware of,' I said. 'Who are you?'

'It matters not who I am, Persephone, but who *you* are.'

I blew out a sigh, then stood up and moved to the next section of flowerbeds, inhaling deeply.

'I have no idea who I am. Nobody will tell me.'

'That's not true. You know you were once married to Hades.'

'Which I find very hard to believe. If you've invented this incredible garden, then you must understand - I couldn't live underground. Nor could I love a man whose world is death.' I gave a little shudder as I spoke.

'No. Your powers do not lend themselves to death,' the voice agreed.

'Exactly. All I want to do is plant things, give them life and watch and nurture them as they grow,' I said happily, tracing the petals of a tall sunflower. 'That's the opposite of death.'

'Indeed.'

'And anyway, I don't have any powers,' I said.

'Persephone, you can do anything you want to do. You have no idea of your potential.'

I rolled my eyes. All my life mom and dad had gone on about my 'potential.' It was nothing but a word thrown around by parents with kids who were failing. Shame fizzed through me again. Y*ou're a failure and everyone knows it.*

'Why do you care about me?' I asked.

'You have been wronged, little goddess.'

'Goddess?'

'Eat the pomegranate seed, Persephone. You'll see.'

The garden around me faded, and my eyes flickered open with a start. These were definitely not ordinary dreams, I decided, blinking up at the star-covered rock ceiling. It really was quite pretty, I thought absently, trying to replay the conversation I'd just had before I fell back to sleep.

Was it Hades? I didn't think so. The voice sounded nothing like him, and I couldn't imagine him creating a garden like that. *Zeus?* Zeus hated me. And wouldn't be so gentle, I was sure. *Then who?*

I woke early the next morning and had a long bath. My muscles ached and the hot water felt good. After navigating my huge wardrobe and managing to select something to wear and dress myself without Skop sneaking a peek, I sat down at my dresser to try one of the hairstyles Hedone had taught me. I wanted her to be impressed when she arrived.

'What do you think would happen if I ate the pomegranate seed I won?' I asked Skop.

'Why would you go to all that trouble to win a seed and then just eat it?' he asked, his voice incredulous.

'Just answer the question.'

'I don't know, but I doubt you'd sprout a tree from your ass,' he said. I shook my head, rolling my eyes but unable to hide my smile.

'Thanks, that's really helpful,' I said sarcastically.

'Maybe if you win another one you could find out, but you only have one at the moment.' He made a good point, I thought. *'What made you think of eating it?'*

'We eat them back home,' I said defensively.

'You eat seeds? Humans from the mortal world are weird,' he said.

'How come the gods stay here in Olympus and don't do anything in my world?' I asked him.

'Beats me. Mostly I ignore the gods, and concentrate on my own shit.'

'Which is?' I asked, raising my eyebrows at him as I fiddled with a lock of white hair.

'Screwing, primarily,' he said, his tail wagging and eyes gleaming.

'I should've guessed,' I said, rolling my eyes. 'You look too cute like that to be so disgusting.'

'There's nothing disgusting about sex. If you think there is then you've been doing it wrong.'

'Eew,' I said, turning away from him. Truth was though, I didn't know if I'd have gotten as far as I did on that cursed bridge without the randy little kobaloi. I was becoming a little bit fond of him.

Hedone arrived a short while later, and to my delight she was very impressed with my hair and make-up efforts. She took me to a grand dining room, very Greek in style with fluted columns everywhere, and high glowing ceilings. A long table set for twenty ran down the center of the room, and we sat together as she took me through the correct order to use knives and forks and spoons and little bowls. I tried to tell her about the movie Pretty Woman, but she just smiled politely at me. I spent the next hour trying to bury an increasing feeling of homesickness, and concentrate on what she was teaching me. Eventually she announced that it was time for lunch, and that she would be back in a few hours.

'And I'm bringing Morpheus with me. He says he knows of somewhere he thinks you might like.'

'Oh, thank you,' I said. 'I assume I'm not going to be dumped on an unsuspecting Hades for lunch again,' I joked awkwardly.

'Err, no, but your presence has been requested by someone else.' She gave me an uneasy smile.

'Who'

'Zeus.'

SIXTEEN

I uncrossed and recrossed my legs under the table, looking around at the ridiculous opulence for what must have been the hundredth time. The moment Hedone had stopped talking, bright white light had consumed me, and then I'd found myself in this grand dining room. Only the word 'room' didn't really apply. There were no walls or ceiling, and stunning pastel colored clouds swirled above and around me. A gentle, temperate breeze swept through my hair, and I closed my eyes. It felt incredible. I was outside. Properly outside, where the air moved, and the sky stretched on forever.

The floor was made from the same white marble I'd seen so much of, as were the columns that ringed the circular space, but gold vines with tiny little white flowers wound their way around them. I'd walked as close to the edge of the room as I dared, but it turned out I wasn't over my last brush with heights, and dizziness swamped me before I could see anything. So instead, I'd sat back down at the table. Steaming hot coffee had been poured for two, and I picked the cup in front of me up and sniffed it. It smelled divine, and I was sipping at it before I could stop myself. A small happy moan escaped my lips.

'You humans and your coffee,' said a voice, and Zeus shimmered into existence in the chair opposite me. He was in blonde surfer boy form. Fury filled me instantly.

'Hello,' I said stiffly. 'I've been wanting to have a talk with you, so I'm glad you've invited me to lunch.' He smiled at me, and my heart skipped a beat. I couldn't pretend he wasn't obscenely gorgeous. *He abducted you. He's an asshole.*

'So I heard. Shame about yesterday's Trial. I understand you missed out on a room with a view?' I said nothing, just sipped more coffee, letting my anger bubble. 'What do you think of the view here?' My eyes dropped to the table, shame pricking through my anger. I was instantly annoyed with myself for giving my emotions away. 'Ah, but of course,' Zeus said softly. 'You won't be able to go close enough to the edge to see.'

'As if you didn't already know that,' I spat. 'You've done this deliberately, to mock me.' I glared at him, projecting as much venom into the look as I could.

'You and I have gotten off on the wrong foot, Persephone,' he said softly.

'The wrong foot? Explain to me how there could possibly be any other kind of foot? You kidnapped me!'

'That was when I thought you were just a useless little mortal human. I can see now, you may have lost your powers, but you kept your spirit.'

I stared at him, confused.

'You're saying this *after* I failed to cross the chasm?' I would have expected that to cement his poor opinion of me.

'You were clearly terrified, yet you tried anyway. I admire that.' I frowned suspiciously. 'Let me show you the view, Persephone. This might be the only time you're off Virgo for a little while, and I believe you will appreciate the... openness of my realm.'

'Your realm? Where are we?'

'Leo. Sky realm of Zeus, center of Olympus,' he smiled at me. Power emanated from him, and my anger was melting away. I knew, vaguely, that he was doing it, but I was struggling to care. 'We are in my personal rooms at the top of Mount Olympus. The citizens of my realm live in houses that float in the ring of clouds around the mountain, or further down the mountain itself. And they get around in wooden ships with sails powered by light.' I stared at him. 'Now tell me, surely you want to see that?' His voice was warm and seductive and I couldn't deny that what he had described sounded amazing.

'OK,' I said, standing up. Zeus stood up too, then held his hand out towards the edge of the room. Glass appeared out of nowhere, wrapping itself around the marble floor and stretching up.

'You can't fall, I swear,' he said to me, then strode to

the glass. I followed him cautiously. The dizziness didn't come as I got closer, and I wondered if that was because of Zeus, or because I knew I couldn't fall. Either way, I got close enough to the edge to see beyond.

And Zeus was right. The view was spectacular. If I'd had any lingering doubt that this was all in my head, it would have been dispelled at once - there was no way I could have invented what was before me.

Beyond the circular room was a thick band of fierce black clouds, crackling with purple electricity, but nestled in amongst them were massive mansions. Many had walls made entirely from glass, presumably so that they could make the most of the view of the mountain I was on, and all had elaborate courtyards filled with greenery. In the gap between the clouds and us were four of five of the ships Zeus had described. They were breathtaking. Reminiscent of pirate ships from movies back home, they were slightly different shapes and sizes, but all had taught metallic sails that sparkled and shimmered like liquid gold. I couldn't stop staring at the one closest to us, the colors of the pastel clouds reflecting in the rippling surface.

'They're beautiful,' I breathed.

'I know. And they are a functional way to move between the realms. My daughter Athena is very good at creating things of both use and beauty.'

'Athena created them?'

'Yes. Along with your mortal world.'

I snapped my eyes to his.

'Athena created humans?' Zeus barked out a laugh.

'No, no, no. That was myself and my old friend Prometheus. Athena created the mortal world, where your precious New York is. Last time the Olympians fought she convinced me that humans should not pay the price of our disagreements, and I allowed her to create your world to put most of them. You know, as an experiment.'

'An experiment?'

'Yes. Humans are more resourceful than I realized though. The last lot managed to break the boundary into our world. Athena was most upset when I scrapped it all and she had to start again.'

My mouth fell open.

'What-' I started, but he waved his arm dismissively.

'I'm hungry,' he said.

My mind still reeling from what he had just said, I followed him dumbly to the table. *Scrapped it all and started again?*

'I'm sensing that you don't have a particularly high opinion of humans,' I said, sitting down.

'They have their uses. And we have many half human demigods here in Olympus. In fact we even allow them in the academies to learn to use their powers.'

'So humans can live in Olympus?'

'Not unless they are born here. Which many are.' He pulled a face, and snapped his fingers. A plethora of fruit appeared instantly on the table, all laid out on shining silverware.

'So, if I were to win these Trials, I still wouldn't be able to live here?'

'If you were to win, you would be reinstated as a-' he faltered, looking up at me as he leaned over to reach a platter of watermelon.

'A goddess?' I asked, thinking of what the voice in the garden had said last night.

'Hecate told you?'

I said nothing as the god shrugged. *So it was true. I used to be a goddess.* A shiver ran through me and I did my best to keep my face impassive.

'It doesn't matter if you know. The point is, I've changed my initial way of thinking.'

I raised an eyebrow at him, then reached for a bowl of grapes.

'The mighty Zeus admits he was wrong?' I said carefully.

He laughed, and it was a happy sound, that made me feel warm and safe.

'No. But all beings, great and small, are prone to changing their minds.'

'Meaning?'

'Meaning, I want you to win.'

'Look, I'm really confused,' I said, my brain bursting with questions. 'You brought me here to upset Hades, right? Because he doesn't want me here. When you abducted me,' I paused to glare at him, 'what were you hoping to achieve?'

'Honestly, I didn't really think it through,' he shrugged, the mischievous gleam back in his eye. 'I didn't even expect to find you.'

I sighed, and rubbed at my forehead.

'Where's Skop?' I asked, suddenly realizing my kobaloi guard was nowhere to be seen.

'Oh, I didn't think he needed to intrude on our lunch.' Suspicion burned through me.

'There's not much point in me having a guard if you can dismiss him,' I said.

'I'm the Lord of the Gods. Dionysus's lapdogs will do as I bid them.'

Arrogance and annoyance were written across his face as he began to eat the fruit he'd gathered onto his plate. I matched his silence as we ate, thinking hard. So far, he had been more forthcoming in his answers than I had expected. I needed to get as much information as I could out of him. And though my anger was difficult to hold onto, my distrust of him had gone nowhere. Clearly his powers had missed that emotion.

'So, I get my powers back if I win?' He nodded at me. 'It seems like Poseidon wasn't a fan of me. Will he object to that?' Zeus made a pffff sound.

'Poseidon is a cautious old man, who gives himself too much to worry about. And Hades' unlawful actions have brought about a word of trouble for him too. Ignore him.'

'Why does he think I'm dangerous?'

Zeus looked at me, and the fruit suddenly vanished. In a heartbeat, it was replaced by mountains of pastries, the smell divine. He reached for something covered in shining chocolate.

'You know I'm not going to answer that,' he smiled. I picked up a donut, covered in powdered sugar, and bit into it. It tasted even better than it smelled. 'I like watching you eat,' said Zeus, and my eyes snapped to his. Energy rolled off him, and it was infectious. It seeped into my own body; life and ferocity building inside me like the purple sparks in his eyes. 'I like to see a woman as beautiful as you enjoying using her senses.' His voice was low and husky, and heat flooded my core.

He abducted you! He's a god! You're not really feeling these things! The voice in my head was screaming at me, and I forced myself to listen to it.

'Is there any way I can get my powers back?' I blurted out.

'No,' he said simply.

'Please? I'd have a better chance of winning.' As I said the words, I wondered why I wanted them so much. I didn't want to win. I wanted to go home.

'No.' I let out a little snarl of frustration and Zeus smiled. 'You are quite, quite beautiful,' he said.

'Will you at least tell me what they were?' I snapped, ignoring his comments, and my rising body temperature, as best I could.

'No. I'm inclined to let your frustration build a little longer. I think watching you-' he paused, eyes boring into mine, 'explode,' he said slowly, and every muscle in my body clenched, 'would be very pleasurable indeed.'

'Send me back,' I said quickly. 'I want to go back to my room now.'

He reclined in his chair, a lazy smile on his beautiful face.

'Very well. Thank you for the pleasure of your company today. I'll see you soon,' he said, and the white light flashed.

SEVENTEEN

For a long time after I was safely back in my room, I couldn't help feeling like I'd just lost some sort of game. It made me furious that he could manipulate my body like that. Thank god my brain was harder to coax.

'*You know, he thinks he's the big cheese, but he's not. That's why he's so pissed at the moment,*' snapped Skop. He was really not happy about being left behind. I was surprised he was taking his guarding duties so seriously to be honest.

'What do you mean?' I asked the kobaloi.

'*Oceanus is back. Which means Zeus is no longer the strongest being in Olympus,*' he said cattily.

'Oceanus is stronger than Zeus? What do you mean he's back? Where did he go?'

'*Gods, you're clueless,*' he sighed, and flopped onto his front paws. '*The Olympians went to war with the Titans,*' he said, and I nodded.

'I remember learning that. Cronos was told that his own son would overthrow him so he ate all his children.'

'Correct. Fucking weirdo. But his wife, Rhea, hid her seventh son, Zeus. He grew up, rescued his eaten siblings, then the war began.' I opened my mouth to ask how you could rescue someone who had been eaten, but closed it again. I wasn't sure I wanted to know the answer. 'The Olympians won, and threw most of the Titans into Tartarus, a pit of endless torture. But some Titans didn't fight, including Oceanus and Prometheus. Two of the most powerful beings to have ever lived. Titans are the original gods, they're fiercely strong.'

'Oh,' I said.

'The Titans who didn't fight were allowed to live in Olympus, as long as they kept to themselves. Which they did, but everybody knew Zeus feared and hated them. They were seen less and less, and eventually they just vanished. Until recently, when Oceanus returned.'

'Why did he come back?'

'Some descendant of his went and woke him up, is what I heard. But he was good mates with Hades back in the day, and they've fallen in together again pretty quickly.'

'So that's why Zeus is so angry? He's scared?'

'I wouldn't say it to his face, but yeah, that's what I think.'

'How do you know all this stuff?' I asked him.

'Parties. Everything you need to know can be learned at parties. They're where all the politics of Olympus are

managed.' I thought about the ball, supposedly my biggest
Trial yet.

'That's what Hedone told me.'

'She's right. As well as smoking hot,' Skop said. I rolled
my eyes, even though I agreed with him.

'The masquerade ball can't be as bad as the chasm,' I
asserted, loudly.

'I wouldn't be so sure about that,' Skop replied.

A little while later there was another knock on my door
and I jumped to my feet to open it. I was bored, and pent-
up; anxiety-fueled energy was surging through me. The
fresh air in Zeus's realm had only served to remind me
that I was trapped underground here, and I was becoming more and more bothered by the fact.

'Good afternoon, Persephone,' said Hedone, but I
looked straight past her at the man behind, towering over
her shoulder. He must have been at least eight feet tall,
and just like me he had a shock of white hair. But he also
had white eyebrows, over sparkling blue eyes and his skin
was a very pale blue. Glittering dust seemed to swirl
across his face as I stared, and he smiled at me, a broad
smile that made his incredible eyes light up even more.

'I'm pleased to meet you, Persephone. I'm Morpheus,
god of dreams and permanent resident of the underworld,' he said, and held out his arm around Hedone.

'Hi,' I said, and took his proffered hand. His skin was
ice cold and smooth, and I noticed he was wearing

something that looked like wizards' robes, a gaping sleeve falling back and revealing deep blue swirling tattoos snaking up his muscled arm as he shook my hand.

'The lovely Hedone tells me you're missing your garden.'

Alarm bells rang in my mind. This man was the god of dreams, and he knew I was missing gardens. Did the voice in the garden in my dreams belong to him?

'I am,' I said.

'Well, I haven't sought permission from the boss, but I think I know a place you might like,' he said with another broad smile. His voice sounded nothing like the one in my dreams.

'Thank you,' I said. 'Can we walk there, instead of doing that flashy thing?'

He laughed, and his skin seemed to ripple with more blue light.

'Of course.'

We walked for ages, and I checked with Skop that he was paying attention to where we were going again. The thought of getting lost in this underground labyrinth was more than I could take. Hedone walked with her hand in Morpheus's and they frequently exchanged happy glances with each other.

'Are you two, um, an item?' I ventured awkwardly.

'Yes,' Hedone beamed at me. I thought about that for a moment. The goddess of pleasure with the god of dreams. I bet that lead to some seriously epic sex.

'So, Morpheus, do you control everyone's dreams?'

'Oh no. No, I create themes for people's dreams, then I allocate them as necessary.'

'Themes?'

'Yes. Like fear, or self-reflection, or guilt, or humor. Every individual interprets those themes differently, in their sleep. The sub-conscious is a powerful thing, and it dictates most of my work.'

'Can you... can you talk to people in their dreams?'

'Oh yes. But I'm only allowed to do that on order of Hades.'

'Oh. Can Hades do it too?'

'All of the Olympians can. They can do pretty much anything they like,' he said, with a raised eyebrow. 'Are you getting a visitor in your sleep?'

'No, no, I'm sure it's just an overactive imagination,' I said quickly, and Morpheus lips quirked into a smile.

'Well, whatever it is, it's nothing to do with me, I can assure you,' he said.

'Huh. Will you be at the ball?'

'Of course. Are you prepared for it? I've heard the tests are going to be good,' he said.

'What have you heard?' said Hedone, excited. 'You must share!'

'That would be cheating! I could lose my job,' he said teasingly, then leaned forward and kissed her quickly. 'Sorry, my love.' I felt a stab of jealousy at their cute flirting and squashed it guiltily. Hedone was nice. Why would I begrudge her anything?

'Persephone has a little more prep to go through, but

mostly just conversational etiquette now,' Hedone said. 'She'll do great.'

I smiled warmly at her.

'I'll be honest, I don't see how it can be worse than the chasm,' I said quietly. Neither Hedone or Morpheus replied.

'*Told ya,*' said Skop in my head.

We walked the rest of the way in silence. The path was on an incline, with small sets of steps interrupting the blue torch-lit corridors at regular intervals. We must have passed a hundred doors, until eventually we stopped in front of one.

'This room doesn't get used any more, as far as I know,' said Morpheus. 'But Hades used to use it a lot. Anyway, there's some sort of magic still infused into the room and some of the plants have survived without company.'

'Plants?' My heart skipped a beat. There really were plants in this place?

'A few, yes. We call it the conservatory.' He pulled on the door handle and held it open for me, gesturing into the room. I stepped hesitantly through the doorway.

Something inside me sparked to life as I cast my eyes around the derelict room. It looked just like I would expect a conservatory to look, if it had been neglected for fifty years. The walls and domed ceiling were made of glass, presumably to let the dull light in, and beautiful once-white wrought iron bars curved up and around the whole structure, creating the frame that supported it. But my attention was drawn to the one color I had rarely seen since coming to the underworld. The one color I was always most drawn to. *Green.* Twenty feet away, sprawling and out of control was a giant yucca plant. Its long leaves were droopy where they should have been sharp, but they were still vibrant with color. I moved further into the room quickly, looking for other signs of life. I found two more yuccas, a fair few succulents, low on the ground in moulding soil, and to my sheer delight, right at the back and leaning keenly towards the weak sun, a single orchid.

'How on earth have you survived?' I murmured to it as I crouched down, inspecting it closely.

'It's nothing to do with earth, I assure you,' said a slithery voice, and I leapt to my feet, my stomach lurching.

'Hades!' I heard Morpheus say, his voice filled with surprise. I turned to see him hurrying towards me, a smoky cloud forming before him. 'I'm sorry boss, I didn't know you would be here.' He was talking quickly, his smooth demeanor and confident grin gone.

'And why, exactly, *are* you here?' Hades' voice made my skin crawl, as though something cold was slithering all over me.

'Persephone was missing her plants. I thought this place might cheer her up.'

The smoky form was now humanoid, though void of features as always. Hades said nothing, and I looked for Hedone. She was nowhere to be seen.

'Since when have you befriended this human,

Morpheus?' asked Hades eventually. Morpheus dropped his gaze to the dirty floor.

'I was just doing a favor for someone. I didn't think it would do any harm. I'm sorry, boss.'

'Leave,' Hades said. Morpheus turned and I hurried towards him, trying to skirt as far around Hades as I could. 'Not you, Persephone,' he said though, as I drew level with him. Fear and something unidentifiable skittered through me on hearing him say my name. Morpheus threw an apologetic glance at me over his shoulder, then disappeared through the open door. I gulped. 'I heard you had lunch with my little brother,' Hades said. *Oh god. This could get awkward.*

'Not through choice,' I replied, trying to keep the wobble from my voice. There was a pause.

'Did you enjoy it?' My eyebrows shot up in surprise. Not only was it not the question I was expecting, but the tone of his voice had changed. The iciness was gone, and he sounded almost nervous.

'It was nice to feel the breeze on my skin,' I admitted. 'But I dislike Zeus intensely. So no.'

To my astonishment, Hades chuckled.

'Good. I dislike him intensely too.'

'So I've heard,' I said cautiously.

'I...' Hades started, then tailed off. 'I never thought I would see you in this room again,' he said eventually, quietly. The slithering was gone from his voice completely, his tone now rich and deep. This was nothing like the way he had been with me at the end of our last conversation. What had changed? Suspicion filled me, and despite my efforts to ignore it, so did hope.

'It doesn't surprise me that I've been here before,' I told him. 'I feel something strong about this room. But I don't know if that's just happiness to see something growing.' Hades snorted.

'I wouldn't say growing. More like *not dying*. It takes all my power just to keep that one damn flower alive,' he said, and a smoky arm gestured at the orchid. 'The other plants are feeding off the residual magic left over I think.'

He was keeping the orchid alive? I definitely hadn't expected that.

'Well, it's beautiful,' I said carefully, stepping back towards the orchid. It was too. It was a slipper orchid, the shape of it round and sensual. It was a vivid purple, with yellow accents softening the petals.

'You planted it,' he replied, his words barely audible. Something pulled at my gut, and for a brief second I felt something so strong it took my breath away. It was a desperate, desperate desire to be somewhere, but I didn't know where.

But the feeling ebbed away fast, and was replaced with that same crushing sense of being trapped. Not physically trapped here in the underworld, but trapped somewhere deeper and infinitely more painful. I felt separated from my own emotions, and I knew I was being kept apart from something more important than anything else I knew. Was it him?

'Why did you send me away? What happened between us?' I asked quickly. 'It's killing me not knowing.'

I looked pleadingly at where I knew his face was, flashes of silver cutting through the dark smoke.

'Nothing happened between us,' he answered, his voice sad. 'Circumstances beyond my control meant you had to leave.'

He didn't hate me. Relief and happiness crashed through me, at the same time as my rational brain screamed at me. *Why do you care? You don't know this man, and he's made of fucking smoke and death!* But rational thoughts were no good to me here. When I wasn't around Hades, the thought of ever being with him was intolerable. But once I was in his presence...

'Hades, I need to know what happened. Please, give me my memories back.'

'I can't. It is not safe.' Exasperation filled me, and I clenched my hands into fists. 'But, if it helps, I'll stop making your life harder,' he said gently. I raised my eyebrows. I didn't even know he could speak gently.

'How?'

'Well, for a start, I'm sorry I got angry with you before. Hecate kind of threw me through a loop. I wasn't ready to see you alone. I'm normally excellent at controlling my emotions, but you're...' I waited, my breath held. He shook his smoky head and carried on. 'You're the one thing my asshole brother knew would cause me pain.'

'Pain? I'm sorry,' I whispered. And I was, though I wasn't sure why.

'No, I'm sorry. You didn't choose any of this. It's my fault. And to say sorry, I'd like you to have this room.'

'Really?'

'Yes. Just until you lose the Trials and go home, that is. You must understand how important it is that you don't stay here.'

A flicker of indignation ignited in me, and I spoke before thinking the words through.

'If what you're saying is true, why don't you want me to be your wife again?' Saying the word wife out loud felt weird and I instantly regretted it.

'Persephone, please. I can't answer that.' His voice was strained, and I felt a little guilty about pushing him when he was clearly making an effort.

'Fine,' I muttered.

'Good. In the meantime, take care of that fucking flower for me so I don't have to.' My eyes flicked between the orchid and him and I couldn't help grinning at him.

'Why are you suddenly being nice to me?'

Hades blew out a sigh, the smoke around his face rippling.

'Seeing you here, in this room... It's impossible not to be. And if you are only to be here a short while longer, then you may as well enjoy it.'

'Thank you, Hades,' I said sincerely.

This time I saw more than a flash of silver. Hades solidified, and I swear, my knees actually went weak, like I was in a slushy romance novel.

He was *beyond* beautiful. His eyes were swirling liquid silver, and the emotion pouring from them was written across the rest of his face. Jet black hair curled past his ears, and he had a thick covering of dark stubble spreading across his chiseled jaw. His lips were soft and full and parted slightly. My eyes darted down his body, taking in a black shirt stretched tight across massive shoulders, open at the neck and showing a smattering of curly chest hair, a heavy duty leather belt, and ripped navy jeans.

I don't know what I'd expected Hades to look like under the smoke, but my gods, it wasn't this.

'I'm sorry,' he said quietly, and I watched the words form on his lips, before his image vanished under black smoke again. 'I struggle to control myself around you.'

'Please,' I half-squeaked. 'Please, stay like that, instead of the smoke.'

'No. I must go.'

'Wait, before you do,' I said quickly. My heart was racing. 'Have you been talking to me? In my head?' The smoke flickered.

'I want you to lose the Trials, but I don't want you to die doing so,' he answered eventually.

'Is that a yes?'

'Goodbye, Persephone. Enjoy the conservatory.'

The smoke vanished.

EIGHTEEN

I stared at the empty spot Hades had vanished from for a long time. Emotions were crashing around in my head, that feeling of being separated from something rising and falling inside me. It didn't matter what Athena had said, I couldn't ignore my past. Not when I was apparently now living in it again. I almost wished I hadn't seen Hades under the smoke, because now that I had, I couldn't get his image to leave me. Those fierce cheek-bones, sensuous lips, his bulging chest... Every other man I had ever seen paled into nothingness next to him. And it was more than physical attraction. I knew him. I knew that offhand humor, that rich version of his voice.

He kept the orchid alive for you. It's all he had left.

I knew that's what the flower meant. What this room meant. And he had known when I entered it today. *He still cares.* Then why did he want me to lose? Surely, if he had another chance of being with the woman he didn't want to leave in the first place, he would welcome it?

What had happened? Why had I been made to leave? Frustration welled inside me.

It wouldn't work. I didn't want to live underground, in a place with no proper outside, and a glass conservatory the only garden I could access. I didn't want to be tied to a man whose dominion was death. I didn't want to live in a world without windows, for gods' sake. He may be beautiful, and I may have a connection to him, but whoever I'd been when this was my home, I wasn't that person any more.

Hades was right. I should try to enjoy the time I had here as best I could. I scanned the room, looking for a trowel. I spotted a pile of tools stacked against the glass, and when I went to investigate I found a rusted faucet on the end of a creaky copper pipe in the ground. Good. I had everything I needed to immerse myself in a few hours of gardening, and try to forget about this crazy infatuation.

Skop tried to talk to me a few times while I worked, but I gave him one word answers. Before long I had managed to lose myself to the soil, and the hours flew by. Too soon, Hecate came into the room, telling me it was time to train. I reluctantly left the conservatory with her, half listening to her berating me for getting my nice clothes 'covered in crap', but mostly just trying to keep Hades' face from invading my mind.

'I saw Hades today,' I told her, after we had beaten the

shit out of each other for an exhausting hour, and were tucking into roasted beef in my room.

'Oh?'

'And I mean, I saw him. Like under the smoke.'

'Ohhhhh.' She looked at me, a wicked gleam in her eye. 'I knew he'd slip up if he spent enough time around you.'

'So is that his true form then?'

'No, if a god showed you his true form you'd die, you're human. But it's the non-lethal version of it.'

'Oh. What does his true form look like?'

'Erm, glowy. And sort of terrifying.'

'Right. So, do you see smoke Hades, or...' I paused, trying to think of what to call non-smoke Hades.

'Hot Hades?' offered Hecate. That worked, I thought, nodding. 'I see hot Hades. Everyone who lives or works in the underworld does. But Virgo is one of the four forbidden realms. Hades is by far the most secretive and private of the Gods.'

'So, he must not be enjoying all this Trial stuff being shown to everyone?'

'No. He's not. The gods ran a competition for Immortality a while ago, and each god hosted a Trial. Hades tried to refuse having his here on Virgo, but Zeus made him. And I think that's why Zeus is making him hold his Trials for a wife here. Because Hades made it so clear he didn't want to do it before.'

'Zeus really is a dickhead,' I said.

'Yup.'

'Why does he dislike Hades so much?'

'That's a really long, difficult question. And one Hades could answer better himself.'

'Huh. Maybe you should set up another date,' I said teasingly, but I half hoped she would say yes. I was longing to see him again, even though I knew I shouldn't.

'No way, the ball is tomorrow night, and you don't need any more distractions.

'Fine,' I said on a sigh.

'Hedone is having a dress and mask made specially for you, they'll be here tomorrow.'

'OK.'

'And make sure you take your dagger. It's the only weapon you have that will work against gods, remember that.'

'Why would I need to harm a god?' I asked her, alarmed.

'Persy, are you learning nothing? You must always be prepared.'

I slept badly that night, and for the first time I didn't visit the beautiful garden with the Atlas fountain. Part of me wished I had. Its calming serenity was just what I needed, even if I didn't know who was taking me there. I sighed as I rolled out of bed, the ceiling lit with the daylight glow telling me it must be morning. The last three or four times I'd woken it had still been covered in twinkling stars.

'So, what's the plan for today?' asked Skop, yawning.

'Finalize the food for the feast, and go over greeting and conversational etiquette,' I told him with a scowl. My idea of a nightmare. If I had my way it would be beef burgers and a cheerful hug, but apparently that didn't cut it if you were trying out for queen of the Underworld. 'I hate this place,' I muttered as I stomped into the bathroom and started the water running in the shower.

'It's not that bad. You know, I was thinking that you should name that dagger Hecate made for you.' I gave him a look from the bathroom door before I closed it and pulled off the long silk camisole I'd slept in.

'Why?' I asked him mentally as I stepped under the water. I instantly felt less bad-tempered, the weary grogginess dissipating as the water flowed over me.

'Because all proper weapons work better if they have names. Hecate made that blade for you, it's one of a kind. And probably magic. You might be able to bond with it if you name it.'

'Oh. OK. What shall I call it?'

'Name it after something you love. Or miss.'

'Light,' I said immediately, without thinking about it. 'I'm fed up being underground.'

'You didn't like it much better outside,' Skop retorted.

'That does not count as outside. Zeus's place had a proper outside. Wherever that chasm is...' I tried to think of a word for the still, temperature-less, beige void but gave up.

'There's plenty of light down here.'

'Not real light.'

'Fine. How about... Faesforos?'

'What does that mean?' I asked, and repeated the word aloud. I liked how it sounded.

'It means bringer of light,' Skop answered. A little shiver ran through me, although the water was still hot. Bringer of light. *'Maybe you can bring some real light to the underworld,'* he said.

'Do you think I can win this, Skop?' I asked him slowly.

There was a long pause.

'I know there's more potential in you than you know there is,' he said eventually.

There was that fucking word again. I hated it. *Potential.* Always so much potential, but never, ever fulfilled.

'I thought you were here to offer comedic relief,' I sighed. 'Not deep and meaningful pep talks.'

'Your wish is my command. Did I tell you about the time Dionysus tricked Poseidon into having sex with a tree?'

The rest of the day with Hedone flew by. The ball was starting at eight, and she'd packed the day with last-minute preparations. To my delight, she had decided to celebrate my human, mortal heritage by serving a feast of food from my own world, specifically New York. Hot-dogs, pastrami sandwiches, smoked salmon bagels, cinnamon rolls, powdered donuts, and more were on the menu, and for the first time I actually began to look forward to the party a little bit.

That was until I had to start practicing how to greet people. Hedone had persuaded Morpheus to assist, and he entered the grand doors of an empty dining hall over and over again for an hour, looking surprised and delighted to see me each time. My acting skills were no match for his though, and my awkward hand shakes and uneasy smiles were not up to Hedone's standards at all.

'Watch me do it, darling,' she told me patiently. Morpheus left the room, then re-entered, a cocky look on his handsome face.

'Morpheus, it's such a pleasure to see you,' enthused Hedone, stepping towards him and holding out her hand. He took it gracefully, bending and kissing it.

'I'm honored to have been invited,' he said.

'But of course you were! And may I say, you look magnificent. How are your family?' She managed to keep her voice sincere and sultry, and her eyes were fixed on his the whole time.

She turned to me. 'You see, Persephone? Don't sound bored, don't sound over-excited. Just try to be elegant, and regal. Don't shake hands, hold yours out to be kissed, like you're more important than they are.'

I frowned. This was so not my thing. Like not even close. But it was one evening, then it would be over. I could do it.

'Right,' I said.

'Always ask about their family, and never forget that flattery will get you absolutely everywhere in Olympus. Try to pick out something specific to compliment your guests on.'

'OK,' I nodded. 'Let me try again.'

Eventually Hedone decided she was satisfied with my level of 'enthusiasm and sophistication'. I felt like a total fake, but she said my carefully plastered on smile was acceptable, and I was willing to accept that she knew best. We ate a brief lunch, consisting mostly of fruit, 'so that we had room for the feast', then we went through table etiquette again, followed by socially acceptable levels of swearing. Apparently the Olympians were entirely exempt from these rules, but the rest of us were expected to abide by them.

'There is one more thing I wanted to talk to you about,' Hedone said to me as we walked back to my room.

'Sure,' I said.

'It's about... well it's about sex.' I stumbled slightly as I looked at her in alarm.

'I'm not expected to-' I started, but she waved her hands quickly.

'No, no, of course not. But you should be aware, when lots of beings with powers get dressed up and drunk together, sex is pretty inevitable. And I don't believe attitudes to it here are quite the same as you'll be used to.'

'Please tell me I'm not attending an orgy,' I groaned. Hedone gave a tinkling laugh.

'No, although they're pretty frequent too. But gods, and demigods for that matter, are very good at disappearing for a short while, then reappearing later.'

'So you're saying that if someone vanishes, they're probably at it somewhere?'

'Yes. Part of the game at these parties is watching for who disappears at the same time.'

'It sounds like bad reality TV,' I muttered. Hedone gave me a small frown, then continued.

'Zeus and Apollo are probably the worst for it, and if Hera is present it can cause sparks to fly. One of your jobs as hostess is to cover for people who have irate or worried partners.'

My mouth fell open.

'I have to cover for folk cheating on their partners? No!'

'It's all part of the politics, I'm afraid. And when Aphrodite does her thing, nobody is really to blame anyway.'

I thought about how Zeus had affected me the previous day, the desire my traitorous body had felt. Did Aphrodite do the same thing?

'Can the gods make someone have sex with them, even if they don't want to?' I asked, aware that my voice was betraying my fear. That was seriously not OK.

'Technically, yes, but it is strictly forbidden.' Some relief washed through me. 'You must remember that gods have enormous egos. Most will try to win you over. There is no satisfaction in taking something they haven't won.'

'What did you mean by Aphrodite doing her thing?'

'Ah, she would never make anyone do anything against their will,' Hedone smiled at me. 'Quite the opposite. Her presence tends to exaggerate all desires. A tiny crush or curiosity becomes heightened. Hence an increase in wandering eyes and hands.'

That sounded dodgy as hell to me, but I said nothing.

'You'll get used to our ways, I'm sure,' Hedone said as we reached my door. 'Try not to worry, and if you can, try to enjoy it.' She laid a hand on my shoulder and I felt a surge of gratitude towards her.

'Thank you so much, for all your help. You really didn't need to give me so much of your time,' I said. An oddly bitter look flitted across the beautiful woman's face.

'Time is a funny thing,' she said quietly. 'Good luck, Persephone. I'll see you tonight.'

NINETEEN

'You can do this,' I breathed, brushing my hands down my skirt for the hundredth time. I was standing before an enormous stone archway sealed with deep purple drapes, and I was starting to struggle with my nerves. The memory of me clinging to the bridge, sobbing and shaking, kept interrupting my confidence, and the longer I waited the more I just wanted the big entrance part to be over and done with.

The main counter to my last public failure, and the reason I wasn't already a quivering wreck, was my absolutely unbelievable outfit. Hedone had freaking excelled herself, and I was positive that I'd never looked so good. To be honest, I probably never would again, and I was determined to enjoy it while it lasted. The dress was another fitted halterneck but this time with no plunging neckline, rather it tied around my throat. There was no back to the top of the dress at all though, the fabric of the skirt resting perfectly across the small of my bare back, then falling to the floor. The skirt itself was made up of hundreds of flowing ribbons of chiffon, all overlapping and slightly transparent, and they parted tantalizingly when I walked, showing flashes of skin and making my legs feel a million miles long. But my favorite thing about it was the color. Every ribbon making up the skirt was a different shade of green. The deepest reminded me of evergreens and Christmas, and the lightest was a powdery teal. When I moved the colors blended and merged, making it look as though the dress were alive. The bodice was white, and tiny green flowers snaked up and around my ribs, accentuating the shape of my breasts. Long, ridiculously soft white gloves covered my arms, reaching well past my elbow and making me feel Marilyn Monroe levels of glamorous.

I had fixed my hair in an elaborate style involving lots of curls and braids, and the white ringlets that fell about my face to my shoulders made the black mask around my eyes stand out even more. There was something thrilling about wearing something so delicate, yet fierce. It looked and felt like it was made from lace, and magic kept it perfectly on my face, un-moving. The lace pattern was of tightly weaving vines, and a swirling green feather stood up proudly on the right side of the mask, forming a statement flourish. I loved it. I had also strapped *Faesforos* to my thigh, as Hecate had instructed me to. I would have preferred it to be strapped to my ankle, but I was wearing the gold, heeled sandals that criss-crossed their way up my calf again, plus the dress would have revealed the weapon. I wasn't especially comfortable having a blade that close to my important parts, but I trusted Hecate enough to risk it.

'I think this is it,' said Skop beside me, as the drapes rustled. My heart rate quickened, my palms beginning to dampen as I realized he was right. The curtains were opening.

'Citizens of Olympus! Please welcome your hostess for the evening, Persephone!' But the commentator's words were lost to me as the room beyond the curtain was revealed. Hedone had told me what she had planned, but I could never have imagined something so utterly stunning.

The room didn't look like any of the others I'd seen in the Underworld so far. Its vaulted ceiling was twinkling with stars, and the huge space was dotted with Greek columns, but the similarities ended there. There were no windows, but the walls were the same as the ceiling, deep navy and sparkling with stars. It was as though the floor was floating in the night sky, but I wouldn't have described the room as dark. Atop all of the columns were flames, burning in various colors and casting a soft glow over everything. They were seemingly staying put by magic. Running from the archway I was standing in all the way across the room was a long red carpet, ending at a raised dais. The gods' thrones were all present, and all empty. But the room itself was far from empty. Everywhere I looked I could see people and creatures all dressed in beautiful, grand clothes, and every one of their imposing, masked faces was fixed on me.

Shit. I dropped hurriedly into a curtsy, and a slight applause rippled through the crowd. I took a hesitant step into the room.

'*Fucking own it, Persy,*' said Skop's voice in my head. I raised my chin and took another step along the red carpet. If I was ever going to walk a red carpet, it would be looking like this I thought. My confidence grew the farther into the stunning room I got. The columns were short enough that the torch-light carried, but tall enough that they were still grand. Delicate gold vines, with little buds that glittered like diamonds, wound around them, reminding me of Zeus's dining room. They were perfect for breaking up the large space, and hiding behind, I thought wryly. Satyrs and tiny women I assumed were nymphs moved between the guests holding trays of drinks and tiny canapés, and the whole room smelled divine. Kind of like strawberries but musky. Excited energy thrummed through the air, an anticipation that was almost tangible. When I judged that I was in the middle of the long carpet, I paused and turned slowly on the spot, making a show of scanning every one, and squashing the relief I felt when I spotted Hedone and Morpheus. *Channel what Hedone taught you,* I thought. *A little arrogance, a lot of grace.*

'Thank you all so much for joining me tonight,' I said loudly, and a touch aloofly. 'I am honored you have all made it. Once I have a drink I will be happy to receive you all.' A satyr appeared out of nowhere, holding up a saucer-shaped stemmed glass full of clear liquid. 'Oo,' I said, my formality slipping. 'Thanks.' He grinned at me, then shot off towards the back of the room, between the legs of the silent crowd. I took a grateful sip of the cool drink, a delightful fizz lingering on my tongue.

I could do this.

One by one the guests approached me, and I soon became very grateful for my gloves. There were only so many people you wanted to kiss your skin, and some of the guests were positively freaky looking. I had no idea what they were, but many seemed to be hybrids of animals, and a fair few had wings. The majority looked human though. I kept my practiced smile plastered on my face, and complimented most people on their masks. They were all so striking that it was hard to focus my attention on anything else. I tried to remember everyone's name as they introduced themselves, but it was impossible to keep them all straight.

'Are you remembering all these names?' I asked Skop silently, as I drained my glass. The satyr appeared immediately with a new one.

'*I already know most of these douchebags,*' he muttered back. '*None of them have recognized me though.*' He had a mischievous tone, and I sent him a warning glare.

'Don't fuck this up for me, Skop. It's serious.'

'*I'm glad you finally think so,*' he answered.

After fifteen minutes of introductions a gong sounded, and a hush descended over the room.

'Honored guests, citizens of Olympus, please welcome your gods!' sang the commentator's voice, and white light flashed over the dais, drawing everyone's attention. The room as a whole dropped to their knees, and I followed suit quickly. I only lasted a heartbeat before lifting my bowed head though, my eyes seeking out the one god I really wanted to see.

Hades was in his smoke form, of course, but like everyone else he was wearing a mask. *And he was letting his eyes show through it.* They fixed immediately on my own, and my breath caught as my emotions responded automatically. Something deep and true and almost painful flowed through me and I grasped unsuccessfully at the feeling. Too soon his eyes flicked away from mine and I released a ragged breath, before realizing that his mask was incredibly similar to mine. It was jet black and the same shape, but I didn't think the pattern was vines. I was too far away to tell. Had Hecate done that on purpose? Where was she? I scanned the other gods as they gazed over their assembled crowd. Aphrodite stood out the most, in a completely sheer gown that had a hint of pink to it, her skin the color of chalk and her hair and lips a vibrant red. Hera was dressed far more conservatively, in a teal toga that made her dark skin glow, but her mask was the most elaborate, an enormous peacock feather fanning up and over her piled-high up-do. Zeus was sporting an older look today, dark hair shot through in the right places with gray and a traditional toga that showed off most of his taut, muscled chest.

'Thank you for attending. Please announce the first test of the evening,' Hades said, his voice the nasty slithery one. My skin crawled and I screwed my face up in conflicted confusion before a loud noise drew my attention behind me. Shimmering into existence with a scraping sound was a giant hourglass. The top half was filled with sand, but it wasn't falling. Apprehension trickled down my spine like ice.

'Tonight Persephone will face three tests,' boomed the commentator, and I realized with a start that the cheerful blond man was standing a few feet from the hourglass. 'And the judges will decide whether you get zero, one or two tokens.' Two? The leader only had five, and I already had one. Wait, why was I excited? I didn't want to win, I reminded myself sharply. Lose, but don't die. That's what Hades had said. So far nothing felt particularly lethal about the ball. 'There are a few rules that apply to the whole evening, so let me make those clear.' He looked intently at me. 'You may not ask for direct help with a single test. If you require information, you must acquire it naturally via conversation, or that test will be forfeit.' I nodded. 'You may not leave the ball.' I nodded again. 'And you may not drop any of your duties as hostess. If at any point you are deemed to be behaving inappropriately, the test will be forfeit.'

'Understood,' I said.

'The first test is a scavenger hunt,' he beamed, looking around at the whole room again, and there was a smattering of applause and excited chatter at his words. I narrowed my eyes suspiciously. I was pretty good at those as a kid. 'Persephone needs to find four clues, that will lead to a key to unlock the hourglass. If the hourglass runs out, then that test is over and lost.' Why would I need to unlock an hourglass? A sick feeling gripped my stomach, and my breath became shallow as something began to shimmer inside the large hourglass. No... Surely they wouldn't... To my horror, the shimmering stopped, leaving a man standing in the bottom half of the hourglass. He was dressed in a simple toga, and didn't look more than my age. His eyes were closed and he appeared to be asleep. A trickle of sand began to fall from the top of the timer, running off his dark hair onto the bottom of the hourglass. 'Here's your first clue,' the commentator said, and a small scroll appeared in my hand.

'You can't do this!' I said, ignoring the scroll and turning to the gods. 'What happens to him if I fail?'

'What do you think? Could you breathe if you were drowned in sand?' answered Zeus lazily. Bile rose in my throat and my head swam slightly. No, this wasn't fair.

'These Trials are supposed to be dangerous for me, not people I've never even met!' I exclaimed. 'Let him go!' I heard gasps around me, and Athena stood up. She looked identical to when I'd first seen her.

'Persephone, the ways of Olympus are new to you, but you can not change them. The only way to save this man is to complete the test. You are wasting time.'

I gaped at her.

'*She's right. Get the fuck on with it,*' said Skop in my head.

'Your little pet can't help you on this Trial,' said Poseidon suddenly, and Skop gave a little yelp of pain.

'Leave him alone!' I shouted.

'Yeah, leave off,' said Dionysus indignantly. With a little flash, Skop vanished and reappeared by Dionysus's side and a tiny bit of relief washed through me. The wine god would look after him.

But now I was on my own and a man was depending on me for his life.

TWENTY

My hands shaking, I passed my glass to the little satyr who was hovering next to me, then unrolled the scroll that had appeared out of nowhere. There were two lines written on it.

Adorned with a blue feather and lined with white lace
This is a magnificent way to hide one's true face

I read it twice. It had to be referring to a masquerade mask, surely? So I just needed to find one matching the description. A blue feather and white lace. I looked around the room. Everyone was staring at me. I heard a loud cough, and spotted Hedone giving me a pointed look. *You must carry out your duties as hostess or the test will be forfeit.* The commentator's words rang in my mind, and I scrambled to remember what I was supposed to do once everyone had arrived.

'We shall be seated for food in one hour!' I said triumphantly, as I remembered what I had been taught. 'Let the music commence!'

The melodic sound of a harp filled the space, and I turned in surprise. The thrones had vanished from the dais and now a beautiful woman with silver hair was teasing the delicate tune from a harp twice the size of herself. But she didn't have a mask with a blue feather and white lace, so I dragged my attention from her. Eyes flicking to the unconscious man in the hourglass, sand beginning to pool at his feet, I set off towards Hedone.

'Good evening, Persephone,' she said formally as I reached her.

'Good evening,' I replied.

'Were you able to receive everyone before the gods arrived?'

'No, not even half. But I am on my way round the rest of my guests now,' I beamed, as people began to crowd around me. I turned, the smile still fixed on my lips. I scanned their masks, trying to slow my heart rate. No blue feathers. *Shit.* I held my hand out to each in turn, thanking them for their attendance, letting their names go in one ear and out of the other, before hurrying on. I managed to spot a few blue feathers, but none of the masks had white lace on them. It sounded like a feminine mask, so I started trying to approach women more. Skop could have really helped out here, I thought ruefully.

Just as I spotted a lady in a puffy pink dress that I had

yet to talk to, I felt gooseflesh raise on my bare skin. I turned around slowly, already knowing what had caused the temperature to drop.

'Hades,' I said, as I came to face-to-face with his smoky form.

'Persephone,' he replied, his silver eyes swirling. My rational thoughts scattered.

'You look...' I trailed off, biting down on my lip as I struggled to find a word to finish the obligatory compliment.

'Smoky?' he offered. My mouth quirked into a smile at the unexpected comment.

'Yes. Smoky.' I felt my shoulders relax a little.

'If this wasn't being broadcast to the whole of Olympus, I would have been willing to lose a bit of the smoke.'

There was no ice in his voice.

'Why do you not let them see what you look like?'

'The King of the Underworld isn't especially popular. They expect a monster, so I give them one.' His swirling shoulders shrugged.

'But... You're not really a monster?' I asked hesitantly. *Hopefully*. Hades paused before answering.

'I'm every bit the monster they believe me to be.'

Part of me didn't want to believe him, but the memory of when we had first met, the screaming, burning bodies and the blood, filtered through my mind. He was the lord of the dead. Surely monster came as part of the package. I mean, these gods put innocent people's lives in danger for entertainment, I thought, glancing at the man in the awful hourglass against the far wall.

Couples had begun dancing to the harp music in front of him, as though he was just part of the decorations. I shuddered.

'I... need to greet everybody,' I said. I wanted to ask Hades if he'd seen a mask with a blue feather and white lace, but I was pretty sure that would earn me a disqualification and seal the poor man's fate.

'Of course,' he said, inclining his head slightly. 'You-' he faltered. 'You look incredible.'

'Oh. Thank you,' I said, unable to stop the wave of happiness that spread through me at his words. *Totally inappropriate happiness,* I scolded myself. *Seriously, get your priorities straight!* I turned away from him with an effort, looking for the lady in the pink dress. I spotted her, but when I introduced myself I could see that she was wearing a matching pink mask around her bright blue eyes.

'Hello,' said a woman's voice as a beautiful tan-skinned man with short dreadlocks apparently called Theseus took my hand. I nodded politely at Theseus and turned to the voice. Red mask. Dammit.

'Good evening,' I smiled at her. She was wearing a skin-tight scarlet dress, had ink black hair and she was beautiful. 'Thank you for attending tonight. Your dress is lovely,' I said.

'Well, it's not like I had a choice in attending,' she said with a smile that stopped before it even reached her cheeks. 'I'm Minthe.'

'Oh!' *Minthe as in the current forerunner for Queen of the Underworld?* What the fuck was she invited for?

'Apparently it's good form for me to show up. And to be honest, I wanted to find out what all the fuss was about,' she said, looking me up and down with a sneer on her face. All my bully alarms sounded at once in my head. Instinct made my shoulders start to contract and my eyes drop to the floor. As they did though, I caught a glimpse of my shining gold sandals, and the liquid like movement of my skirt. I looked fucking awesome, I remembered. And this was my damn party. 'As I expected, I don't really get why you're such a big deal,' Minthe said, in a bored voice.

I raised my chin slowly, forcing my shoulders back. The satyr I was coming to love appeared at exactly the right moment, and I swiped a saucer glass up from his tray.

'Ditto,' I said simply, then took a long swig from the glass. 'Do enjoy your evening,' I said coolly, then strode away from her, as her expression morphed into a scowl. I desperately wished Hecate was there to high-five me, or at least Skop to call Minthe something rude, but the surge of pride I felt was enough for now. I knew her sort through and through. And instead of cowering, I had held my own. I could do this.

When I finally spotted the woman in a mask with a blue feather and white lace, another ten minutes had passed and the sand was up to the unconscious man's thighs. I babbled my way through greeting the petite brunette, who was called Selene apparently, scrutinizing her mask closely. A rich blue feather curled from the left side of her mask, standing nearly a foot high, and a complex border of white lace rimmed the mask itself. It was very pretty, but I realized with a lurch that I had no idea what I was supposed to do now that I'd found it. *Just ask her! Ask her for the next clue!* But what if that counted as inappropriate and I was disqualified? I couldn't take risks like that with someone else's life at stake. 'That's a stunning ring,' I said on auto-pilot, pointing at an enormous milky-white gem on her delicate finger, while I scrabbled for an idea of what to do next.

'Why, thank you,' she beamed at me. 'It's a moonstone.'

'How lovely,' I replied. Were her words a clue?

'Here, why don't you try it on?' She slipped the ring off, and I started to tell her that it would never fit on my finger, when I noticed the slightly intense look on her face.

'Thank you,' I said instead, and held out my hand. With a little poof, the ring turned into another scroll the second she laid it on my palm.

'You're welcome,' she beamed at me, then turned away, to talk to her handsome partner. I hurriedly unrolled the scroll.

Standing out in a room full of regular shapes
  This unusual vessel will hold that made of grapes

. . .

Made of grapes must mean wine, I thought. And a vessel would be a goblet or glass. So I was looking for an unusually shaped wine glass? I instinctively looked over at where Dionysus was surrounded by tall women, his black sequined shirt catching the torch light. He hadn't even got one button done up on it, and I couldn't help the little smile that sprang to my lips. Skop was at his feet, and from where I was standing it appeared that he was looking straight up a pretty dryad's skirt. I rolled my eyes, then scanned their hands. All their glasses looked normal to me.

I strolled casually amongst the guests, smiling and trying vaguely to recall their names as I peered at the glasses in their hands. I didn't remember seeing one odd-shaped glass so far this evening. With a nervous look back at the hourglass, I thought hard. Where would I find the most wine glasses? The kitchens?

It took me a few moments to work out where exactly the serving satyrs and nymphs were appearing from and disappearing to, but as I watched I realized that one of the walls of the room had no twinkling stars at the base, rather a mass of shadow that obscured any details. I approached slowly, and to my fascination, the closer I got, the less I could see.

'I have a way with light and shadow,' said a silky smooth voice, and a very tall man stepped out of the darkness. He was at least eight feet tall, but impossibly slender. He had onyx skin, a bald head, and was wearing a long black robe.

'I see you wear the color black well,' I said politely. He inclined his head at me.

'Can I help you?' he asked.

'Oh, I, erm, wanted to check on the serving staff.'

'Why is that?' He tilted his head at me, his dark eyes probing. I found him distinctly unnerving.

'A good hostess likes to know that she's on top of everything,' I smiled. 'I don't believe I'd had the pleasure of your name?'

'I am Erebus,' he said.

'Persephone,' I replied, holding out my hand. He didn't take it, so I retracted it awkwardly.

'Erebus,' I repeated, wracking my brain. 'I am new to Olympus, so forgive me if I'm wrong but, are you the god of darkness?'

'And shadows, yes,' he said.

'Do you live in the underworld?'

'I do. Hades is my master.'

'So you must be following this competition keenly,' I smiled.

'The whole of Olympus is following this competition keenly. They are starved for entertainment.' His tone was dry and sarcastic, and it made me want to step away from him.

'Well, I must get on and check in with the staff. It was a pleasure to meet you,' I said.

'You will need permission to cross the shadows.'

'Oh. And who would grant me that permission?' I asked tightly, knowing the answer, and feeling irritation grow inside me.

He gave me a creepy smile.

'That would be me.'

There was a man drowning in fucking sand behind me, and this idiot wanted to play games? I plastered my most ingratiating smile across my face.

'May I cross the shadows, please? I would like to check on the feast plans and stock of wine.'

'But of course you may,' he gestured at the void in front of me.

'You have my gratitude,' I lied, and stepped into the darkness.

TWENTY-ONE

I blinked, the light bright after the gentle ambiance of the ballroom, and the pitch darkness of the shadows. Just like kitchens would have been at a function in my world, long stainless steel counters were covered in bowls and platters, and there was activity everywhere I looked. Nymphs and humans alike, wearing white aprons, spooned food into dishes, bustling back and forth between the counters and a huge bank of clay ovens at the back of the room, shouting to each other over the sounds of clanging and more chatter. I inhaled deeply, and to my delight smelled hot-dogs. I looked to my right and saw rows and rows of different glasses laid out, with more nymphs filling them fast with different drinks, before servers refilled their trays. I walked over to them, my heels clicking on the tiled floor.

'Excuse me,' I said, and the pink-skinned nymph I addressed looked up from pouring a bottle and squeaked.

'I didn't mean to startle you,' I said quickly, as she spilled something blue and fizzy onto the counter.

'What do you need, my lady?' she said, avoiding my eye, and mopping quickly at the spillage.

'It's an odd question, I'm afraid, but do you have any strangely shaped wine glasses?' Her eyes snapped to mine and she tilted her head.

'Actually, yes. It was brought in here about half an hour ago. We thought it must belong to someone here, as it's not one of ours.'

'May I see it please?'

'Of course, my lady.' She hurried away behind a row of tall metal cabinets, and returned less than a minute later with a *square* wine glass. The base, stem, and cup all had perfect right angles.

'How peculiar,' I said, taking it from her. Her mouth fell open when it vanished with a poof, a little scroll replacing it. Relief and excitement tingled through me. *Two down, two to go.* 'Thanks for your help,' I grinned at the nymph.

'You're welcome, my lady' she said nervously as I turned and raced back towards the wall of shadows I'd entered through. I unrolled the scroll as I went, reading quickly.

This week's most desired thing of all
There's no other way to get to the ball

. . .

No other way to get to the ball? I crossed through the shadows, and for a brief second it was impossible not to notice how beautiful the ballroom looked with its soft, glittering light and stunningly dressed guests twirling and swaying to the music. I forced my attention back to the scroll. The most desired thing just this week? What would people want this week that meant they could get to the ball? The answer came to me immediately. *An invitation.* It had to be. I scanned the room for Hedone, and my heart did a little leap when I finally spotted her and Morpheus talking to Hecate. My friend looked knockout, in a white leather catsuit that looked like it had been painted onto her skin, and neon pink shot through her high ponytail. She looked like something straight out of the eighties. I hurried towards them.

'Persy!' she exclaimed when I reached her, and leaned forward to give me a kiss on the cheek. Was that allowed? Hedone hadn't covered that. I glanced at the sultry goddess and she gave me a reassuring smile. 'You look sexy as fuck!' Hecate exclaimed, holding me at arm's length and looking me up and down. I beamed at her.

'I'm glad to see you, Hecate,' I said formally. Hecate rolled her eyes.

'Oh gods, you gotta be all proper here. Rather you than me.' What I wanted to say was, *'they put an innocent man in a fucking hourglass and they'll kill him if I don't win a stupid game, what the fuck is wrong with you people,'* but instead I gave a little shrug.

'You did warn me,' I smiled. I had to word my next question carefully. I didn't want to break the rule about asking direct questions, so I'd already come up with a bullshit reason to ask for what I needed. 'Hedone, I never got to see the invitations for the ball and I just want to double check what time they said the first course of dinner was. You don't happen to have one on you do you?'

Hedone gave me an apologetic smile, and looked down at her slinky black dress. It made her look as curvy as that damn hourglass.

'Nowhere to put an invitation in this dress,' she said, her husky voice somehow accentuated. 'Sorry.' Just as my heart began to sink, Morpheus spoke.

'I have one,' he said, and reached into the inside pocket of his navy blue dinner jacket. He was one of a handful of people wearing clothes from my world. He frowned as he dug about, and I held my breath hopefully. 'Aha!' he said eventually, and passed me a black piece of card.

'Thank you!' I said, and before I could read the gold embossed words, the invitation vanished with a poof, a fourth scroll in its place. Hecate raised her eyebrows at me, and I gave her a quick smile. 'See you at dinner!' I said, and moved away from them, unrolling the paper. My heart was beginning to beat faster now. I was three clues down, and that last one was the easiest yet. I looked over at the man in the hourglass. The sand was past his hips, and fast approaching his chest. I looked back at the scroll, a surge of adrenaline sharpening my focus.

. . .

Serene and melodic, giving spirits a lift
   Apollo and Hermes gave the world this gift

I couldn't help the groan that escaped my lips. The last three clues had been quite obvious but this one... Serene and melodic suggested music. I looked up at the dais. The harp player had been joined by a plethora of musicians, and I couldn't even name half of the instruments I could see. *Shit.* I was going to have to talk to Apollo or Hermes.

Remembering what Hedone had mentioned about Apollo being as sleazy as Zeus, and recalling the genuinely friendly words Hermes had given me when I'd been introduced to the gods, it seemed clear who I should seek out. I scanned the crowd, looking for the red-haired god. All of the Olympians, other than Hades, stood out - they all glowed slightly and they were all completely surrounded by fawning masked folk. Consequently, it didn't take long to spot Hermes. I smiled and nodded my way through the beings around him, trying not to let my alarm show as I accidentally brushed up against a very hairy thing with ten arms.

'Persephone! Great party,' Hermes beamed at me when I finally got in front of him. His close cropped hair and beard glittered in the low light and his elaborate mask was the same bright shade of red, with a yellow feather. He was wearing a traditional toga in black, that much like Zeus's showed most of his chest. I bowed deeply.

'I am honored to call you my guest,' I said respectfully. He flicked his eyes around at the folk still crowded close to us, and suddenly the chatter of the room fell away. It was like I was wearing earplugs.

'You and I were friends, once. I know you don't remember that, but I won't forget it,' Hermes said, his voice crystal clear and his face open and cheerful. As soon as he finished speaking, the sound in the ballroom rushed back, the string instruments casting a mellow, relaxed tune across the chatter. I smiled at Hermes.

'I was hoping to ask you about the sorts of things you preside over as a god,' I said. I needed to be very careful with how direct my questions were. I didn't think I could ask anything about musical instruments, so I would have to work the conversation around to them. This would be a test of my powers of party conversation, I thought, trying not to roll my eyes. Fucking pretentious asshole gods.

'Fire away,' Hermes said, and took a long swig from a tankard.

'Well, I know you're the messenger god, and that you work for Hades sometimes collecting souls,' I said, reciting what I remembered from my classical studies. 'And I know you're famous for playing pranks.' Hermes chuckled.

'I sure am. That little kobaloi friend of yours is a sprite after my own heart.'

'He's not played any pranks on me yet, as far as I know,' I said.

'No, I don't imagine he's allowed to. But he's got quite a colorful history,' Hermes said, eyes glittering with mischief.

'So, what else are you a god of?' I asked.

'Thieves, and wealth,' he said, waggling his eyebrows at me. 'Your own Hades has access to all the underground minerals and gems though, so he is technically richer than I am. But who doesn't love a little heist now and again?'

I raised my eyebrows at him, trying to ignore the term '*your own Hades*'.

'You'd steal from the king of the Underworld?' Hermes barked a laugh.

'I steal from everyone, dear girl! In fact, I was only made an Olympian because Zeus was so impressed with me stealing from Apollo and getting away with it!'

Apollo? I forced my face to stay impassive as excitement bubbled inside me. Did Hermes steal an instrument from him?

'What did you steal?' I asked quickly.

'His prize cattle,' sighed Hermes, staring wistfully into the distance. I felt my shoulders deflate as disappointment washed over me. 'Those were the days.'

'Oh.'

'He was so mad. I only won him around by appealing to his love of music.'

'Music?' My attention snapped back to the god.

'Yes. I invented the lyre, and played it to him. He

liked it so much he forgave me in return for the instrument.'

'The lyre,' I breathed. That must be it. I turned to the dais, trying to recognize a lyre in the hands of one of the musicians. How was I going to find a subtle way of getting onto the stage and getting my hands on one though? I couldn't even be sure if anyone up there had one.

'Yeah. I made it out of a tortoise shell and bits of sheep gut. I don't reckon any of them up there would be too impressed with that now,' Hermes laughed, following my gaze. His laugh cut off abruptly, and I looked at him as his eyes widened. 'That's just given me a great idea. Watch this,' he grinned. The air over his hands shimmered, and a large empty tortoise shell with slimy red string tied across it appeared out of nowhere. I screwed my face up at the smell, and stepped backwards. 'Sheep gut strings,' he said, his eyes dancing.

'What are you-' I started to ask him, but with another wave of his hand it vanished, replaced by a beautifully carved wooden lyre. There was a yelp and a jarring sound and my attention snapped to the stage. A woman standing amongst the musicians was holding out the tortoise-shell lyre, staring at the red on her fingertips in disgust and confusion. 'You- you swapped them!' Hermes started to laugh, an infectious giggle that I couldn't help emulating. 'That's gross! And completely unfair!' I spluttered.

'It sure is,' Hermes replied, and downed his drink. 'But I also find it highly amusing. I need a new one of these,' he said, raising his empty glass. 'Can I leave you to sort this out? One of the duties of a good hostess is to sort out other god's mischief.' He held the lyre out to me with a wink.

'Y-yes!' I said, doing my best not to snatch it from him. As soon as I touched it, it disappeared with a poof, a small metal orb in its place.

'Aha!' barked Hermes. 'I'm so glad to have helped! It was brief, but a pleasure, Persephone,' he beamed, then strode past me.

TWENTY-TWO

I turned the little metal ball over in my hands, hope and anticipation filling me. Honestly, if there wasn't an unconscious guy drowning in sand, the test would actually have been quite fun. The orb had three simple rings carved around it, but other than that gave me no clues. What was I supposed to do with it?

The clues will lead to a key to unlock the hourglass, the commentator had said. I looked at the hourglass. The sand was just falling past the man's shoulders. The orb didn't look like any sort of key I'd ever seen, but that meant nothing. This place was as weird as weird could get.

I walked quickly towards the hourglass, apologizing to people as they stepped up to talk to me.

'I'm sorry, I won't be a moment,' I said politely, over and over again, causing the time it took me to cross the hall to be doubled. Stupid damned manners. Eventually I reached the hourglass. A hush fell over the room and nerves skittered through me as I looked back over my shoulder. Everyone was watching me, now they had realized where I was going. They knew I had solved all the clues and got the key. There was no way I could do this bit naturally, but surely this wouldn't get me disqualified? The commentator had said I needed to unlock the hourglass. I paused, holding my breath, waiting for his booming voice to reprimand me, but only the sounds of the harp carried through the ballroom. I dropped into a crouch, my relief short lived. The frame of the hourglass was made of what looked like brass, including the thick base which bore a broad plaque in the middle. There were two round holes in the plaque and a short inscription underneath each.

Innocent and *guilty.*

I frowned. What did that mean? Was it referring to the man inside? I stood up, peering through the glass at the man's sleeping face. He had deep creases around his eyes but he was too young for them to be wrinkles from age. He had sandy colored hair that was tidy and short. How was I supposed to know if he was guilty or innocent? And of what? I let out a hiss of annoyance and took a deep breath. There must be a clue somewhere. Even these twatty gods wouldn't make a puzzle unsolvable.

I put my hands on the glass and looked again. He was wearing something around his neck, I realized. It was on a leather band and it was small and metal. Some sort of charm. It looked like... a feather? I squinted, trying to see details through the slightly warped glass as the sand began to cover the man's throat - and the necklace. *It was a dagger,* I finally realized. Why would he have a dagger charm around his neck? Did that mean something in Olympus? I clenched my jaw. As an outsider, I was at a disadvantage, once again. *Think, Persephone.* Daggers are not generally associated with innocence. Could the answer be that black and white?

Discomfort rolled through me at the thought of deeming a stranger guilty of anything. Except these Olympian assholes for making me play their stupid games. I took a deep breath. All this time I had been thinking of the guy in the hourglass as an innocent bystander, put through this for entertainment. But what if the gods were not that cruel? What if they actually had chosen someone who deserved it? Not that I was convinced anyone deserved to be drowned in sand.

With a swift movement, before I could talk myself out of it, I dropped my little orb into the 'guilty' hole. There was a metal rolling sound, and then a click. I stepped back, heart hammering as I watched the hourglass. Slowly at first, then faster, the sand began to move the other way, shooting back up the little gap it had come from, quicker than it should be able to.

'Congratulations, Persephone!' The commentator's voice made me jump. 'You've just saved the life of a convicted murderer!'

'What?' I span around to look at the blonde man, standing only ten feet behind me.

'Part of the Titan Brotherhood, this man killed over fifty others, before he was brought to justice by the magnificent Theseus,' he beamed, and gestured at the gorgeous guy with dreads I'd met earlier. Applause erupted through the room, and Theseus nodded and smiled at everyone, raising his glass. 'We'll have a short break for the feast, then your second test will begin. Enjoy!'

Hecate sauntered over to me, her glass raised, as everyone turned back to their partners, talking excitedly.

'Nice one, Persy,' she said as she reached me.

'He's a convicted murderer?' I gaped at her.

'Yeah,' she shrugged. 'What's the problem?'

I opened and closed my mouth a few times. I wasn't sure exactly what I wanted to say, only that this was all really wrong somehow.

'That's not how we deal with criminals in our world,' I said eventually.

'Well if this offends you, I would discourage you from visiting some of the darker areas of the Underworld,' she said, raising one eyebrow. 'The Olympians are rather well known for their colorful punishments of the guilty.' I blew out a breath, and looked about for the serving satyr. I needed some more of that fizzy wine.

'My lady,' said a little voice, a tray appearing out of nowhere.

'Thank you,' I said, and swiped up a glass. 'How do they know when we want a drink?'

'That's their job and they're good at it. Speaking of

which, you completed the first test fast. The judges should be impressed.'

'Hmm,' I said, taking a long swig of my drink. Thank the gods for alcohol. Although at the rate I was drinking, I wouldn't be sober enough to last all three tests.

Over Hecate's shoulder I saw that lots of round tables had appeared, ornately dressed in scarlet red tablecloths and each set for eight guests. Relief that I'd gone through feasting etiquette washed over me when I saw the number of pieces of silverware surrounding the grand black plates and bowls. A loud gong sounded, and people began to make their way to the tables.

'Top table,' said Hecate, as I moved my head side-to-side, trying to work out how they knew where to sit. 'You're on the top table.' She pointed to an oblong shaped table in the middle of the room.

'Where are you sitting?' I asked her.

'With you,' she grinned at me. 'Perks of being the boss's favorite employee.'

'Thank the gods for that,' I breathed. Having a familiar face nearby would definitely boost my confidence.

'Well done, you said gods!' Hecate clinked her glass against mine with a grin. 'We're making progress.'

'Speaking of the gods... Will they be sat at the top table with us?'

'No, they don't eat with us inferior folk. Feasting with the gods is the highest mark of respect a citizen can be given.'

'What about lunch with a god?' I asked quickly,

thinking of my donuts on Zeus's mountain-top. There was no way he'd have been showing me respect, surely? Hecate laughed, presumably at the confused expression I must have had on my face.

'Don't worry, a god trying to get into your pants over a little light refreshment isn't the same. I'm talking feasting, like this, with all of them.'

'So where do they eat?' I asked as we made our way to our table.

'Who knows? Or cares?' she shrugged, pointing to a chair. I saw a prettily inscribed name card on the onyx colored plate. *Persephone*. Hecate moved to the other side of the table, and sat down but I remained standing, as I had been taught. I needed to greet all of my table guests.

'Persephone, it's a pleasure to meet you,' said a man, reaching for my hand. My lips parted and I felt heat rush to my face as my fingers touched his. He was *gorgeous*. And not mysteriously good looking like Morpheus, or pretty-boy good looking like Zeus, but panty-dropping, mouth-drooling, dizzy-making gorgeous. He was built like a football player, a white shirt emphasizing his broad shoulders, and low slung pants drawing my eyes inexorably to his hips. I dragged my attention back to his face, where his dusty blonde hair curled around his ears and his eyes shone blue.

'H-hello,' I stammered. 'Thank you for coming.'

'Wouldn't miss it for the world,' he beamed, and I swear my knees wobbled. His full lips were mesmerizing. He started to move towards a chair, but I stopped him.

'I didn't catch your name,' I said quickly.

'Oh, I'm sorry, I'm not allowed to tell you.' He gave me an apologetic smile.

'Why not?'

He shrugged.

'Hate the game, not the players,' he said with a wink. My initial captivation with him vanished, and I suppressed a growl. Now what were those bastards up to? Was this part of the test?

One by one people came up to me, kissing my hand or curtsying politely, and none of them would tell me their name. The only one of the five I recognized was the woman who was wearing the mask with the blue feather and white lace on it. I cast about for her name, but there had been so many introductions that evening that I couldn't remember it.

'Let the feast begin!' rang out a voice, and a colorful assortment of fruit suddenly appeared on all the plates. I sat down on my chair, picked the correct fork from the array available, and took a breath. I wasn't going to let my guard down for a second - something was definitely going on here.

TWENTY-THREE

'So,' I said, as cheerfully as I could. 'Where are you from?' I turned to the woman sitting on my right. She was pretty, like everyone at the ball, with tight silver ringlets falling about her shoulders and a flush of freckles across her full cheeks.

'Leo,' she smiled at me. Leo. That was Zeus's realm.

'Are you a goddess?' I asked.

'Everyone here is a god. Except you.' I looked across at the woman who had spoken. She was sitting next to Hecate, who was glaring at her. Her mask was black and red, bold lines breaking up the colors, and I couldn't help thinking of Mexican wrestling masks. She had a mountain of black curly hair piled high on her head, and she was wearing a ball gown that had a perfectly fitted corset to accentuate her massive breasts. It took a serious effort not to stare at them.

'What are you the goddess of?' I asked her with a forced smile.

'Can't tell you that,' she shrugged, and stabbed at a piece of salmon. We'd moved on from the fruit course. 'What is this? Is it from your crappy world?'

I felt my eye twitch, but kept the smile on my face.

'It's smoked salmon. And yes, it's quite popular in the mortal world.'

'Well, it tastes like shit,' she said.

I inhaled slowly through my nose, and turned to the only other man at the table, who had yet to say a word. He was the most unassuming person I'd seen at the ball yet. He was a normal size, was wearing a traditional style toga that didn't show too much of his chest, had close cropped brown hair and a simple silver mask with no feather or adornments. He wore an impassive expression on a forgettable face.

'Hello. Where are you from?' I asked him. He looked up at me from his food, and fire leapt to life inside me. Screams penetrated my skull, distant at first, then louder, as flames licked around my vision. Then as quickly as they'd started, the thoughts receded, leaving me with a white knuckled grip on my cutlery, and no idea what he'd just said to me. 'I'm-I'm sorry, could you repeat that?' I said, blinking, my pulse racing. Had Hades just got angry with someone somewhere? Why would that affect me if he wasn't even here?

'I'm from a place you are as yet unaware of,' the guy said, his expression still neutral but his brown eyes swirling with something seriously other-worldly. Something *dark*. Had he just caused that?

'Oh,' I said, unsure what else to say.

'Gods, you sound so dramatic,' the big-boobed lady said to him, rolling her eyes. The man gave a her a small smile, and carried on eating his salmon. She let out an exaggerated sigh. 'I'll level with you, Persephone, I'm a bit disappointed.'

'I'm sorry to hear that,' I said, trying not to grit my teeth. 'How can I improve your evening?'

'Well, I had hoped Oceanus would be here. There's a big gathering next week, and the rumors are that he's at the center of it all. I wanted to get some inside info.' Her eyes shone amber behind her mask, and the more I looked at them, the more annoyed with her I got.

'I would have liked Oceanus to be here too, but I'm afraid I can't control the Titans.'

'Well you seem pretty friendly with this one,' she said, jerking her thumb at Hecate.

'Wait, what?' I stared at Hecate as she swallowed her mouthful of food and shrugged. 'You're a Titan?'

The big-boobed woman snorted.

'She's one of the most powerful beings in this room, of course she is.'

'Why didn't you tell me?' I asked her. I wasn't sure why it mattered, but somehow it did. I felt betrayed, even though she had no reason to have mentioned her heritage. But the Titans were all supposed to be in a pit of torture weren't they?

'Erm, you never asked? Why does it matter?'

'Oh Hecate, even pathetic mortals from the human world know that Titans are losers,' said big-boobs. I glared at her, but Hecate coughed, and gave me a look.

'I'm descended from Titans, yes. Hades gives a lot of Titans jobs. Let's move on to something else shall we? How's your mother?' She turned to the beautiful man, who was beaming at the hot-dog that had just appeared on his plate.

'What's this?' he asked, looking at me.

'It's a hot dog,' I told him, my face flushing as soon as I laid eyes on his lips.

'What's the yellow stuff?'

'Mustard.' He picked up his knife and a small laugh escaped me.

'No, like this,' I said, and picked up my own hot dog. It tasted divine, and a pang of homesickness bolted through me. *I would be home soon enough.* Everyone around the table picked up their own hot dogs and started to eat, appreciative murmurs ringing through the group.

'Mom's great thanks,' the hot guy said suddenly, turning to Hecate. 'She's been looking forward to tonight. She's got something planned for later I think.'

'Who is your mother?' I asked.

'Ah, lovely Persephone, it seems so mean that I'm not allowed to answer any of your questions,' he said, and something fluttered in my stomach as he gazed at me. 'I guess it wouldn't be cheating to tell you she's an Olympian though,' he said, and winked at me again. *Guys who wink are not your type. Guys who wink are not your type.* I clung to the chant in my head, and gave him a thank-you nod.

'So, you lived in New York?' said the lady in the blue mask I'd met earlier.

'Yes, do you know it?' I asked her excitedly. It was the first time someone had mentioned anything from home to me.

'Yes, very well. It is a realm that comes alive at night.' I liked the thought of New York being its own realm, and I smiled warmly at her.

'Well if you win the Hades Trials, you can kiss goodbye to seeing cities lit by moonlight,' said big-boobs. 'In fact you can kiss sunlight goodbye too.'

Why was this woman being such a pain in the ass? I bet she was one of the ones Hedone warned me about, that would be sneaking off with some married man later on, I thought. I'd be damned if I was covering for her.

The gong sounded suddenly, pulling me out of my thoughts, and the commentator's voice swiftly followed it.

'Good evening Olympus! I hope the guests are enjoying their meals? Well, they're going to have to wait for their desserts, as we have a short interlude... Persephone's second test!' A new hourglass shimmered into existence next to the first, which still had the unconscious murderer in it. I peered at the new glass, trying to see inside. It was much smaller than the first, and it seemed to be empty, until with a shimmer, a woman appeared in the bottom half. She was on her knees, her head lolling to one side so that a mass of dark hair tumbled down over her chest. My gut constricted, and any enjoyment I had begun to get from the ball slipped away, replaced by renewed disgust of these games. It was too easy to forget how fucked up these people were, and I had begun to relax. That was a mistake.

'As you can see, this is a smaller hourglass, and the sand will fall much faster. You don't have long for this test, Persephone.' He beamed at me, then vanished, reappearing with a little flash of light right next to me. I tried to keep my nerves from showing on my face as he handed me a golden orb. 'To complete this test and save that woman's life, you must take apart this key, and match the correct piece to the correct guest on your table. You may not ask any questions at all. Are you ready?'

'Erm-' I said, but before I could finish speaking he cut me off.

'Good, let's begin!'

I instinctively looked at the hourglass, and my breath caught, panic rising in me as I saw how fast the sand was falling. The hole in the middle was larger than the last one, and the base of the hourglass was already completely covered. I didn't imagine that I would have more than five minutes before the sand reached the woman's head. I turned back to the table, lifting the orb to my face. The room was completely silent as I inspected the ball. There was nothing on it all, no markings or inscriptions or patterns. What was I supposed to do with it? The last one had three rings carved into it. I gripped each side in my hand and twisted, imagining the rings on the last orb. To my relief there was a click and I felt movement, then I fumbled with the metal as the whole thing broke apart in my hands. Two pieces dropped onto the table in front of me, hitting my plate with a clang, and I felt my face flush.

Act like you don't give a shit, I thought, trying to channel Hecate's fierce attitude. *It doesn't matter if the rest of Olympus thinks you're clumsy; what matters that you save this woman's life.*

I laid all the bits out on the table, turning them over in my hands and looking for clues. It reminded me of cracking open an Easter egg, the center of the orb hollow. There were five pieces, which made sense as I had five unknown guests at my table, plus Hecate. I was assuming she wasn't part of this test, as I already knew who she was.

'Aha,' I mumbled, as I lifted one of the broken bits of shell to my face, wishing there was more light in the ball-room. Painted on the inside, tiny and delicate, I could just make out a crescent moon. Whipping my gaze out over my silent table guests, I picked up the next piece, looking closely until I found a tiny heart with an arrow through it. I checked the other three pieces as quickly as I could, finding a tiny skull, a cracked bowl, and what looked like a fountain. *Come on Persephone, work it out.* Five symbols and five guests. None of whom would tell me their name or what they were gods of. The guests *must* match the symbols. I turned and looked at the hourglass. The sand was already at the woman's waist. *Concentrate!*

Well, the heart and arrow was the symbol for cupid in my world. I couldn't remember the Greek name for him, but I knew he was the god of lust, and Aphrodite's son. There was no question that he had to be the gorgeous guy, as that would explain the conversation about his Olympian mother, and the fact that I couldn't talk to him without thinking about him doing filthy things to me. I picked up the piece with the heart on it, and held it out to him across the table. He grinned at me as he took it, and the commentator's voice rang out across the room, although I couldn't see him anymore.

'Correct! Eros, god of desire and sex!'

Thank the gods for that, I thought, but felt little relief. That was the only easy one. *OK, what next?* The skull... My eyes darted to the plain guy. The plain guy whose gaze had made me see fire and hear screams. Without giving myself time to second guess my decision, I held out the skull piece to him. His lips barely moved as he took it and the commentator's voice boomed once more.

'Correct! Thanatos, god of death!'

A shiver ran through me. I'd been eating next to the freaking god of death and not known? I pushed the unhelpful thought aside, and picked up another piece. The moon. I looked at the three women, and a memory of a conversation earlier that evening flashed into my head. *'It's a moon-stone,'* the lady in the blue mask had said when I admired her ring.

'Selene!' I exclaimed out loud, as I remembered her name. She said she liked New York because it came alive at night. Surely that would make her goddess of the moon or night? With a deep breath, I passed her the piece of orb with the moon on it. She gave me a big smile, and this time I did allow a little relief to wash through me as the commentator spoke.

'Correct! Selene, goddess of the moon!'

I looked over at the hourglass. The sand was just starting to cover the woman's chest. I only had a few minutes more, I was sure. My palms were beginning to sweat, and adrenaline was making my insides feel like they were vibrating as I picked up the last two pieces. A broken bowl and a fountain. I looked between the pretty young woman from Leo and the big-breasted jerk with the stupid hair, and bit down on my lip. I didn't know what either symbol meant. The bowl was broken... Was there a goddess of broken things? And the fountain... It couldn't be goddess of the sea or water, as that was surely Poseidon? I tried to think of famous fountains, but nothing came to me. What could the broken bowl mean? Could it just represent stuff being messed up? In which case it surely had to be the miserable trouble-maker? *If you get this wrong, a woman dies.* I closed my eyes. I was sweating profusely now. I didn't know what the correct answer was.

TWENTY-FOUR

Go with your instincts, Persephone. The pretty young woman didn't match something broken, surely. But the rude, abrasive woman I could definitely see as broken somehow. With a massive breath, I opened my eyes and held out the broken bowl piece to big-boobs. The scowl on her face as she took it made me sag in relief. If she was scowling then I'd got it right. I turned and passed the last piece to the other lady and she grinned.

'Correct! Eris, goddess of discord, and Hebe, goddess of youth!'

Each of the gods held out their piece in turn, and I watched as they glowed a faint purple, then left their owners outstretched hands and floated towards the center of the table. With a little burst of light they rejoined, but this time the golden orb had the three rings carved around it. I stood up and reached forward, plucking the key from where it was hovering, and hurried towards the hourglass. The sand had reached the woman's shoulders and was only inches from her chin. I dropped into a crouch as soon as I reached the hourglass, looking for the hole to put the key in, expecting more inscriptions. But there were none. I screwed my face up, searching for the place to put the orb.

'Where do I put the key?' I asked aloud, panic starting to flood me as I stood up, scanning the frame of the hour-glass desperately. There were no holes, no inscriptions, nothing. Silence met my question and my eyes darted to the woman's face. The sand was moving past her chin, and would cover her mouth in seconds. 'Where does it go?' I shouted, my stomach tensing so hard it hurt as I started to run my hand over the metal. As my fingertips reached across the top of the hourglass they felt hot and I paused my frantic movements, feeling more carefully. I could only just reach the top, and there was no way I could see what was up there, but I was sure I could feel a channel carved along the edge of the metal. With a last look at the woman's face as the sand covered her bottom lip, I reached up and pushed the key onto the top of the hourglass. I held my breath as I heard the sound of metal on metal, sure it was the sound of the ball rolling. Then there was a clunking sound, and the sand in the timer began to rush upwards all at once. For a second I thought the woman would suffocate from all the sand moving in the opposite direction, but before I could do anything, the bottom half of the hourglass was clear. My heart felt like it was stuck in my throat as I watched her chest, relief making my knees feel weak as I finally saw it move. She was breathing.

A smattering of applause filled the room, and I heard Hecate give a loud whoop. What the fuck was wrong with these people? I clenched my fists at my sides, trying to rein in my emotions. A person just nearly died and they were clapping like they were watching tennis or something? Even Hecate, my only friend here, didn't seem to grasp how messed up this was. *You're in another world now. Just get on with it, and get home.*

I turned, knowing the smile I'd fixed on my face must look more like a grimace, but unable to conjure up anything better.

'This is bullshit,' I said through gritted teeth, hardly moving my smiling lips but needing to say the words out loud. I felt a bit better.

'*I know it is. But you're doing a good job,*' said a voice in my head, and my smile slipped.

'Hades?' I projected the thought at him, using the image of his smoky form to send the word.

'*Yes.*'

'Where are you?' People were tucking into huge bowls of frozen yogurt, and none of them were looking at me anymore.

'*Watching.*'

'Are you coming back?'

'*Yes.*'

'You... you helped me with the other Trials.'

'*Yes. Eat your dessert.*'

I let out a long breath, and walked slowly back to the table.

'Nice job, Persephone,' beamed Eros.

'Thank you,' I said absently.

'Oooh, someone isn't happy with this set up,' said Eris, her eyes flashing behind her mask. 'What's wrong, perfect Persephone?'

'Seriously Eris, give it rest,' said Hecate, rolling her eyes as she spooned yogurt into her mouth. 'Persy, this stuff is awesome, I can see why you miss American food.'

'It is very delicious,' said the woman I now knew to be Hebe. I turned to her, deliberately ignoring the goddess of discord.

'I wonder if you could tell me, Hebe, how does the fountain represent you?' I asked her, politely.

'Oh, it's the fountain of youth,' she said cheerfully. 'A little obscure perhaps, but I'm glad you worked it out.'

'Thank you,' I said, and dipped my spoon un-enthusi-astically into my own yogurt. My appetite had vanished. 'I didn't, really. I just knew you weren't the broken one.' There was a collective intake of breath, and I looked up, directly at Eris. Her expression was dark, her lips twisting in a snarl and venom in her glare.

. . .

A week ago a look like that would have terrified me. A week ago I would have been groveling and apologizing for what I'd said. Hell, a week ago, I wouldn't have fucking said it.

But I was done.

I was angry and scared and sick of being used as a twisted puppet for the entertainment of others, and the only person I could take it out on right now was the bully across the table. So I was going to.

'You're right, I am broken,' Eris said, her voice almost a purr. 'You've no idea how broken I am. And how much I enjoy breaking others.'

'I do have an idea,' I told her. 'I've met plenty of people like you. Hell, I've met quite a few since coming here.'

'Oh naive little Persy. I'm afraid you're wrong. You haven't met anybody as fucked up as me yet. With one exception that is, but you're competing to marry him. So what does that make you?'

Defensiveness sparked in me out of nowhere. Hades wasn't a bully. He may be pretty scary, but he wasn't like her, or Minthe, or Erebus, or Zeus. I *knew* he wasn't. I opened my mouth to respond, but common sense kicked in just in time. I was the hostess of the ball. And Eris was smart as she seemed cruel. I knew what she was trying to do, and I wasn't going to let her bait me into making a scene at my own party. I wasn't going to let her win.

'That makes me a fucking mystery,' I smiled at her, and stood up, pushing my chair back. The whole room turned to me and I raised my glass before Eris could say another word.

'Time for dancing!' I announced loudly, and this time I got an actual cheer, instead of the pathetic applause when I'd saved two people's lives. I needed air, but this stupid underground place had nowhere to go, nowhere to breathe. Claustrophobia began to press in on me, and the rules made clear at the beginning of the evening echoed in my head. '*You may not leave the ball.*' I was stuck here, with all these freaking lunatics. My heart began to skitter in my chest, my breathing too shallow. *Stay calm, don't freak out,* I instructed myself, my eyes darting around the room. There must be a quiet corner I could hide in somewhere. I walked towards the far wall, the one opposite the hourglasses, smiling at everyone I passed as sweat began to trickle down my spine, my anxiety ratcheting higher. I only stopped when I found an area where the columns seemed closer together, and for a merciful moment, I couldn't see anybody. I leaned gratefully against the cool marble of the nearest column, taking a long, slow breath. I probably only had minutes before somebody showed up, but I would take whatever I could get. I just needed a couple minutes to get my shit together, that was all.

If I didn't think too much about the fact that I was trapped underground with a load of well-dressed murderers, then I was OK. But as soon as the knowledge that I couldn't leave worked its way through any positive thoughts I tried to fill my head with, the room seemed to close in around me again. If I was at home and my surroundings got overwhelming I would do what anyone would do - go outside. Get some air. Air. Just a few breaths of cold air to clear my head. But even something that simple was unattainable.

'Stupid, stupid place,' I hissed aloud. 'How the fuck does anywhere not have an outside?'

'I told you, there is an outside. You've been out in it.'

Hades' voice made me jump, and for a split second I thought it was in my head, but then dark smoke rippled in front of me.

'Yeah, on a fucking invisible bridge! What kind of asshole invents one of those? And it's shitty outside, there isn't anything growing, or even a breeze!' I barked the words before he could materialize fully, feeling braver when I couldn't properly see him.

'We don't need a breeze,' Hades replied eventually, a touch of defensiveness to his tone as the smoke stopped rippling, his humanoid form complete. There was no slithering sound to his voice.

'Well I do,' I muttered, casting my eyes down and staring angrily at the floor. A pulsing beat had begun, the melodic orchestra replaced by music far more reminiscent of my home world.

'You are upset?' Hades asked me eventually.

'Yeah. Yeah, I'm upset.'

'Why? You are doing well.' I looked up, searching the smoke for his eyes, as hot tears began to burn the back of mine. Frustration was causing them, and I cursed my body. Tears wouldn't help me, just make me look more weak.

'Who is she?' I asked, my voice barely above a whisper.

'Who?'

I gaped at him.

'Who? Who the fuck do you think? The woman you all nearly killed for entertainment!'

He turned, looking towards the hourglass.

'I don't know,' he said eventually. My mouth fell open, my stomach roiling.

'You don't know? Would you have cared if she had died?'

'No. I do not know her.'

I shook my head, the last of any tolerance I had for this place fleeing me.

'What is wrong with you people? How can you be so self important, so callous, so.... murderous?'

The smoke flickered, and I saw a flash of silver. When he spoke, the iciness was back, and images of snakes poured into my head, my skin crawling.

'You are speaking to the King of the Underworld. Lord of the dead. Ancient and all-powerful and witness to deeds you can't even imagine.' I shrank back against the column involuntarily as the smoky form grew. 'If you had lived through what I have, if you had seen the things my fellow gods have done to each other, have done to those around them... You would hold a different opinion.'

I stared at him. He was blaming the other gods?

'So you aren't as barbaric as them?' I whispered.

'Oh yes, Persephone. Yes I am. In fact, I'm worse than

most of them.' Eris's words flicked into my head. *You haven't met anybody as fucked up as me yet. With one exception that is, but you're competing to marry him.'*

'Why? Do you... enjoy death?' I barely got the words out. I knew I didn't want to hear the answer. Hades flashed solid so quickly my brain hardly registered it.

'I never asked for this role. But it is mine. And I will fulfill it.' What did that mean?

'That's not an answer.' There was a long pause, and I swear he must have been able to hear my pounding heart over the music.

'No,' he said eventually, his voice quiet and the anger lessened. 'I do not enjoy death. But it is my world. It is who I have had to become. If I were as sensitive to it as you humans, I would be a very poor king indeed.'

I frowned, straightening against the column slightly.

'You humans...' I repeated. 'But I wasn't human before.' The claustrophobia pressed in on me again, that feeling of being separated from a part of my own self building inside me. 'I can't have been as indifferent to death as you are. I can't have been.' I could hear the pleading tone to my voice, and I realized at that moment what I was so afraid of, what I feared even more than him and this world.

What if I was once like these people?

This is where I was from, this man was once my husband. Did I ever find entertainment in people's suffering? I felt sick as I stared into Hades' face, and a single hot tear leaked from my eye, sliding down my cheek.

Suddenly, the smoke leapt out from where he was standing, and the next thing I knew I was in a black, hazy bubble. I looked around myself quickly, aware that I could no longer hear the music, or anything else, nor could I see beyond the thick smoke barrier surrounding us.

'What-' I started but my words fell away as I laid eyes on Hades. *It was him*. The real him, under the smoke. My breath caught and desperation filled me as I stared at his face, into his swirling silver eyes. *Home. He was home. He was mine.*

I shook my head, trying to clear the words ricocheting around my brain.

'You were never cruel, Persephone. You were fair and kind and I...' he trailed off, hopeless sadness pouring from his beautiful face. I stepped towards him before I could help myself, and he lifted his hand to my cheek. Ever so slowly, he brushed his thumb across my skin, wiping away my solitary tear. Electricity shot through my body at his touch. His touch was warm, and for some reason I had expected him to be cold. Frustration welled inside me again. I knew so little, and I needed more.

'I hate this place,' I whispered and he flinched. 'Please, please make me understand how this was once my home. Because I know it was. I know you were.'

'It wasn't always like this. It was before you came, and it was again after you left. But when you were here...' His eyes bore into mine. 'You brought light, and life, to a place where I thought none could exist.' He spoke hoarsely, and his words crashed through all the mental armor I'd built up since coming to Olympus.

He loved me. I could see it in his face, hear it in his broken voice, feel it in his electrifying touch. All this time, all those years alone in New York, and someone, somewhere, loved me this much. And I never knew.

TWENTY-FIVE

I stared at Hades, my mind spinning. He was a god. King of the Underworld, Lord of the dead, and he'd just wiped a tear from my cheek.

'Light and life,' I repeated, my stomach feeling like it was filled with butterflies. 'Are those things you wanted here, in this place?'

'Not at first. I just wanted you.' Desire skittered through my core at his words, and I saw his eyes flash with something new. 'Damn Aphrodite,' he muttered. I raised my eyebrows at him and he sighed. 'Her music, her power. She always does this at balls, and the smoke can only keep so much of it out. She's powerful.'

'Love is powerful,' I murmured. The side of his mouth quirked up.

'See? That's her power. Making us both... soft.'

'Soft?' That's the last word I would have used to

describe him. He was wearing the same clothes as he was before, jeans and a black shirt open at the neck. His skin glowed, and I wanted more than anything in the world to touch it.

'Yes. Soft and... passionate. That's what she does.' I tilted my head, trying to clear the image of him lifting his shirt over his taut chest.

'What do *you* do?'

'That's a big question.'

'You won't answer any of my others.'

'That's not fair. I've answered loads now.'

He smelled of fire and wood-smoke.

'You smell like campfires,' I told him.

'Do you like it?'

'Yes.' I stepped closer to him, the low beat of the music filtering through to me now, my hips beginning to sway of their own accord. 'I don't like that I'm not in control of my body though.'

'Aphrodite's power won't make you do anything you didn't already want to,' he said quietly. I looked up into his face. His eyes were alive with hunger now, deep and shining and breathtaking. Slowly, I reached up, and touched his jaw. A thrill pulsed right through my whole body, making all my muscles clench and heat pool deliciously inside me. I wanted him. More than I'd ever wanted anything in my life. He drew a ragged breath, then his hand was on my face, lifting it to his. Our lips met, and fire exploded in my core. Pleasure engulfed me as his tongue snaked between my lips, and desire so strong that I physically ached completely took me over. I pushed my hands into his hair, pulling him into me, desperate to taste him. I was standing on my tiptoes to get as close to him as I possibly could, pressing my body hard against his. His arm wrapped around my back and then he was lifting me, his lips moving from mine and kissing hungrily along my jaw, down my throat. I tipped my head back as I wrapped my legs tightly around his waist, the pleasure from his touch making me tremble. Waves of need pounded between my thighs, and I couldn't think straight as I entwined my fingers in his hair, his lips moving back up my neck.

'I missed you,' he murmured into my skin. 'Gods, I missed you.' A small moan escaped me, even as part of me railed against the fact that he wasn't kissing me for the first time, but I had no recollection of ever having done this before.

'I need you,' I gasped. And it was true. At that moment, I would have done anything in the world to feel him inside me, to meld his body with my own, to find a release for this ferocious desire.

Abruptly, he pulled back, his eyes slightly wild as they met mine.

'But you don't love me.' I stared into his face. The desire I felt for him went as deep as any feeling I'd ever experienced, but love? No. I didn't love him. I barely knew him. And what I did know was conflicted and confusing. I had clearly left too long a pause, as his expression hardened, and he lifted me from his waist, setting me back on my sandals unsteadily. Confusion rolled through me. 'Of course you don't. You are not the woman I married. You are someone new.'

I blinked, my physical response to him making it impossible to work out his words properly.

'I'm Persephone,' I said thickly.

'We must not do this to ourselves. You can't stay here and this would be folly.'

'What?' I felt like I'd been punched in the gut, a hollow feeling of loss and rejection making anger spike inside me, fueled by the passion still making my pulse race. 'You're mad at me because I don't love you? A man I've just met? A man surrounded by death?'

His lips parted and something jet black flashed in his silver eyes. I took a step backwards before I realized I had, the hair on my arms standing up as the temperature plummeted. *It's cold when I'm scaring on purpose*, he had told me.

'And that, little human, is why you can not stay,' he hissed. And I mean hissed, as though he were actually a reptile. The dark smoke around us billowed suddenly, and rushed back towards him, the music and sound of the party smashing into me like a physical hammer.

'Hades!' I shouted, but it was too late. He had vanished.

Unspent desire and tension ripped through me, and I barely contained the scream trying to crawl its way out of my throat as Hecate stumbled towards me.

'I know that smoke bubble,' she slurred. 'You and Hades were getting it ooooon.' She waggled her eyebrows at me, a stupid grin on her face.

'Are you drunk?'

'Yep.'

I rubbed my hands across my face, trying to dispel the lingering taste of Hades, the little pulses of excitement still rippling through me, and the surges of anger and fear that had followed them.

'Hecate, tell me what happened before. Why did I leave? Why did the gods take away all my memories?'

'Persy, please-' she started but I shouted over her.

'Hecate, I'm fucking serious, I've had enough!'

Her face morphed into a frown and she put one hand on her hip.

'It didn't go well with lover-boy then,' she said eventually. I gritted my teeth, exasperation making me feel like my body wasn't big enough to contain what I was feeling. I was ready to fucking explode.

'Tell. Me. What. Happened.' I spat the words out one by one, and Hecate grimaced.

'Alright. But if Hades-' her words were cut off abruptly by the sound of the gong.

'No! No, no, no!' But the commentator's voice bellowed across my fury.

'Is everybody ready for the third and final test? This one's a really good one, I promise you! Where is the lovely lady? Come on over Persephone!'

I closed my eyes, trying desperately to slow my heart rate, to calm down. One more test. Just one more. I had to do this, or some poor bastard would drown in sand. But after that, I wasn't giving up until somebody told me what I needed to know.

I walked slowly and serenely to the middle of the room, trying to look the complete opposite of how I felt. A new hourglass had appeared next to the first two. It was as large as the first one, and currently empty. I glared at it. *And this is why you can't love him*, I reminded myself. He doesn't give a shit about people dying. *You still want to fuck him though,* the contrary part of me chimed in. Stupid damn bad-boy attraction. But I knew, deep down, that it was so much more than that. I'd never felt anything this intense before in my life.

'So, are you ready?' the commentator asked me, from where he stood by the hourglass. I nodded at him. It didn't matter one jot if I wasn't. 'For your third test-' he began, but a resounding crash drowned him out, and everyone snapped their attention to the source of the noise. From the darkness Erebus had been guarding earlier came a flash of orange fire, and a distant scream. *Kitchen fire*, was my first instinct but then I remembered we were in a world of gods and magic. Kitchen fires wouldn't cause this much disruption, would they? There was another flash of fire, then a bird erupted from the shadows and I wasn't the only one who gasped.

Its wing span was massive, easily three times my size, but that wasn't what was most attention grabbing. The whole creature was on fire. It wasn't a bird at all, it was a phoenix, I realized. With a mighty beat of its wings all the tablecloths nearest it burst into flame, and the people stood closest darted out of the way. There was a white flash and Hades' smoke form suddenly appeared in the middle of the room, an arm held high. The phoenix froze in mid beat of its wings, and my heart leapt into my throat.

'What is the meaning of this?' Hades roared, in his cold hissing voice. 'This was not the Trial we agreed upon!' There was another flash of white, and Zeus appeared next to him, his eyes alive with crackling purple lightning.

'Oh but this is much, much better! It appears you have a gatecrasher, big brother. I forbid you to get involved,' he sneered. The temperature plummeted.

'You forbid me to deal with trespassers in my own realm? Who do you think you are?' Hades hissed.

'I am your King,' Zeus replied, growing fast so that he towered over Hades. 'Fill the hourglass! Persephone's new test is to rid her guests of this pest!'

'What?!' I exclaimed, and span to see a tiny form in the hourglass. I swear my heart stopped beating for a second as I recognized the figure.

It was Skop.

TWENTY-SIX

'Wait, you can't expect me to fight that, I'm human!' I yelled, as I turned back to the two gods, the phoenix still frozen in mid-air behind them.

'You are a human competing to become an immortal queen. You will do as you are bid,' said Zeus, his eyes narrowed and a sneer on his beautiful lips.

'Brother, this is too far!' Hades' words had an edge of desperation to them, and Zeus's smile slipped for a beat as he turned to face him.

'You are the one who went too far, Hades,' he said quietly, and fear gripped at my insides as the tension grew between the two gods, venom in their locked gazes. Zeus wasn't going to back down. I was going to have to kill a phoenix before Skop drowned. My throat seemed to lock up at the thought of the kobaloi dying, heat burning behind my eyes again. He would die because of me, because I chose his feather. That wasn't fair, he'd done nothing wrong. His job was to make people laugh, for fuck's sake, why should he be punished for being my friend?

'I'm sorry,' I thought desperately at him, knowing he couldn't hear me but needing to tell him. 'I'm sorry, Skop.'

'*Don't fucking apologize yet, get me the fuck out of here!*' his desperate voice replied.

'Skop! You're not unconscious?' I whirled to look at the hourglass, where he looked for all the world like he was fast asleep, in naked gnome form.

'*It's damned difficult to knock out a sprite completely. My body is useless, but you can't keep a brain like mine down for long.*' My heart swelled on hearing his defiant words, and determination started to battle with my fear. A bright flash made me turn again, and Hera was there between Hades and Zeus, regal and stunning with her peacock feather.

'Enough,' she said, her voice melodic and soothing. 'Olympus is watching, and we have promised them entertainment. Good luck, Persephone,' she said, and then the three of them vanished. I blinked in the bright light, then a wave of heat blasted over me as the phoenix was released from Hades' spell and its huge wings beat towards me.

'*Move, move, move!*' Skop's voice spurred me into action, the shot of adrenaline shooting through my system making me feel sick, but adding a speed to my legs I didn't know I had. All the pent-up tension from my moment with Hades seemed to be pouring itself into my muscles, and I felt strong as I raced towards the stage area, as far from the bird as I could get. It gave a screeching squawk, and then flapped its wings harder, lifting itself high into the cavernous ceiling of the room. What was it doing? I took the few seconds I had with it so far away to study it, searching for any signs of weakness. It was fierce looking, with a bright yellow hooked beak and eyes the same color. The bulk of its body was scarlet red and the flames rolling from its feathered wings burned through an orange ombre to an almost white tip. It straightened in the air, facing me, its massive tail feathers pointing down and flames dancing from them towards the ground. People were scattering across the ballroom, many glowing different colors, and I assumed they were calling their own powers, ready to defend themselves if they needed to. None would be able to help me though. And I had no power. Slowly, I moved my skirt aside, hooking *Faesforos* out of the sheath on my thigh. It felt good in my hand, but as I held it up towards the enormous flaming bird, my positivity took a nosedive. How the fuck was I supposed to use a weapon like this on that? A tiny part of my brain piped up, giving voice to the thought I was trying to ignore. *It's too beautiful to kill.* A mindless skeleton was one thing, but this? It was freaking magnificent. And to be fair, right now it was just hovering, staring at me, doing me no harm at all. Why should I kill it?

'Hello,' I called out to it, trying not to feel stupid. I heard a laugh somewhere in the room. Most likely that big-boobed witch Eris. The phoenix pulsed its wings. 'Please could you leave?' I asked, as politely as I could. This time I heard a louder laugh, and it was male voice. The phoenix's eyes turned inky black suddenly, and a voice boomed through the room.

'You think you can return here, after all these years, and it would be OK? That you would be forgiven?'

My skin felt like it was contracting around me, ice-cold dread trickling through my insides. This person was here for me. And they knew something I didn't.

'I don't know what you're talking about,' I shouted back. 'This is my first time in Olympus.'

'Lies! You deserve to rot in Tartarus for what you have done!'

'I don't know what you're talking about!' I couldn't keep the fear from my voice. My terror was not of the beast before me or the owner of the voice, but of the words he was saying. *What had I done?*

There was a bark of anger, and when he spoke again the voice was a disbelieving hiss.

'If what you say is true, then rather than punish you for your crimes, the gods let you drink from the river Lethe to forget your past? The injustice is unrivaled!' The last sentence was so loud I involuntarily clapped my hands to my ears. The phoenix let out another piercing screech, then dove towards me.

'You need to find whoever is controlling the phoenix

and kill him, you can't stop the bird itself!' Skop's voice sounded in my head as I began to run.

'You can't talk to me, I'll get disqualified and they'll kill you!' I told him frantically. There was no reply, and for a sickening moment I wondered if they had done just that. I skidded as I turned, the phoenix roaring down behind me and I felt searing heat against my back. I pelted towards the hourglass, my worst fears confirmed as I neared it. Sand was falling so fast that Skop would be dead before I reached it. With a scream, I drew the arm back that held *Faesforos* and launched the dagger at the thin glass center of the hourglass, the neck where the two halves met. The sound of metal on glass was followed by a splintering crash, and relief coursed through me. As I'd hoped, I'd hit the weakest part of the structure, and the sand now gushed out of the broken hourglass onto the floor. Skop remained slumped inside but his head was clear of sand. He could breathe. I ducked down as I reached him, only stopping long enough to scoop up my blade from amongst the bits of broken glass, then veered off to my right. I couldn't worry about how the gods would deal with me breaking the sand timer now, I would have to face that later.

Another blast of heat told me the bird was just behind me, and I scanned the room desperately as I ran. Skop said someone was controlling the bird, but who? There were about eighty people here. Could it be Eris, or Minthe, or Erebus? All of them had made it clear that they didn't like me. But that voice... So full of unsuppressed hatred and anger - none of them could have interacted with me all evening and then blown up like this, surely.

My eyes were drawn to the people in the room who were giving off faint light, and there were a number of them, all moving hastily out of my way as I charged through the room, my skirt flying and the phoenix on my tail. I ran past Eris, who was beaming, a deep red energy crackling around her. Even if this wasn't her doing she was enjoying it. I passed Hecate, still standing at the back of the room where I had left her. She had a blaze of purple emanating from her, her eyes milky white. What was she doing?

'The shadows. He's in the shadows.' The voice was faint, but it was Skop's.

'How do you know?' I said, altering my course and heading for the kitchens I'd visited earlier. There was no reply. As I got closer I could see yellow sparks in the darkness, and I raised my dagger arm again. But I must have slowed, because pain lanced through my wrist and I almost dropped *Faesforos* as I looked up. The phoenix had its sharp talons wrapped around my arm, and the breath left my lungs as I was jerked off my feet. I tried to reach around with my other arm to prize the talons off but the bird twisted to the side and I was thrown the other way. We were moving higher, and I looked down at the shadows. The yellow sparks were getting brighter and I realized there was a figure emerging. It was a man, and he looked completely ordinary, save for the murder in his eyes. The power around him could have been fire or energy or electricity, I wasn't sure, but it crackled bright along his skin, leaping and dancing from him like the flames on the phoenix.

'Time to die, Persephone.'

I swung my free arm up, passing the dagger from my immobilized hand to the other, and jammed it as hard as I could into the bird's massive talon. It didn't react. Thinking fast, I tucked my legs under myself and tried to kick out hard to launch myself higher. It worked, giving me a few extra inches to slash at the bit of fiery leg above the black claw. With a squawk, the thing released my arm.

Shit, was all that went through my head as I began to fall, repeated over and over until I smashed into a table. The wood splintered and folded beneath my weight, and for a heart stopping second the tablecloth engulfed me and I couldn't see a thing. I rolled, gasping for the breath that had been knocked out of me, and sending silent thanks that the bird had only lifted me five feet off the ground. Heat sprang up around me as I fumbled my way to my feet, and panic bolted through my body as I saw that the tablecloth still tangled in my legs was on fire. I jabbed *Faesforos* into the material and ripped it quickly apart, stumbling away from it, trying to get my bearings. There he was. The man with the yellow magic, slowly walking towards me.

'Why don't you face me yourself?' I called out, my words coming between gasping pants.

'You're suggesting I'm the coward? You who ran away from the result of your atrocities?' Fury rolled off his words and the yellow energy around him danced out further, but the bird stayed where it was.

'I can't pay for something I don't know I've done,' I said, shifting my weight and gripping my dagger. Fear that he might tell me, and the whole world, what this awful thing was, warred with my need to keep him talking and keep the phoenix at bay.

'You are a murderer,' he hissed. His words hit me like a sledgehammer. No, there was no way that was true. How could it be? I couldn't hurt an insect or plant, let alone kill a person. *You are not the woman I married. You are someone new*. Hades' words sliced through my denial, and bile rose in my throat. Please, please, no. It couldn't be true.

'I don't believe you,' I choked out, and the man bared his teeth at me.

'You took her from me. You took everything that I loved from me.' Pain and grief and madness filled his eyes, and I had no doubt that whether or not his accusation was true, he believed it.

'I'm sorry,' I said, as he reached me. 'If it is true, then I am sorry.'

'It's too late to be sorry! Unless you can bring her back, you must die!' The yellow energy burst out from around him, and agony consumed me. It was like an unending electric shock ripping through my muscles, causing spasms so violent I couldn't stand. But before I could fall to my feet his arm shot out, and he grabbed me by the throat, holding me as I jerked and screamed. 'You deserve worse than this.' I barely noticed as he sucked in air through his teeth, drew me closer to him, then spat on me, his saliva sliding down my cheek. Through the blinding pain, I was only able to process one thought. *Make it stop.* Everything else inside me was shutting down, but my survival instinct was refusing to give up. My arm was rising inch by inch. As the man's eyes blazed with retribution and the pain intensified so much I could no longer see, I buried *Faesforos* into his ribs.

TWENTY-SEVEN

He dropped me with a gurgled shout, and I slammed to my knees with a hard crack that I barely registered. I fell forward onto my hands as my stomach began to heave. I didn't know if I was sick from the pain, or from the fact that I'd just stabbed a man, my head was spinning so fast. I tried to gulp down air between retching, the pain subsiding but my vision still blurry. *Murderer.* He had called me a murderer. I couldn't be and yet... I'd just tried to kill him. *He was going to kill you!* The rational voice in my head tried to drown out the guilt and fear, but it couldn't. I couldn't live with myself, I couldn't draw breath every day, knowing I was the reason somebody else wasn't. *Please, please don't let him be dead*, I prayed, turning my head towards him slowly. He was on his back, dark red blood pooling under one side of him. I crawled towards him, tears filling my eyes.

'I'm sorry, I'm sorry, I'm sorry.' The words tumbled

from my mouth, tasting like the acid that filled it. He groaned and I paused. Then he moved, rolling onto his uninjured side. *He was alive.* Thank the gods, he was alive. I sat back on my heels, letting the tears come. 'What did I do?' I croaked. 'Tell me, who did I take from you?'

'My wife,' he said, his voice hoarse. 'You killed my wife.'

A light flashed so bright that pain seared through my head again, and for a moment I was sure I was going to pass out. I had reached my limit.

'No!' A female voice shouted, and I blinked furiously, trying to clear the tears and blurriness from my eyes. Slowly, the room came back into focus.

Athena was standing before us, in front of smoke Hades and Hecate. Purple energy still rolled off Hecate, and Hades was three times his normal size and his smoke seemed to be vibrating.

'You must be judged, Persephone. The Trial is over,' Athena said, her voice like a balm to my pain, calming my mind. The three judges shimmered gently into existence before me.

'But what about him? You have to help him!' I pointed desperately at the man bleeding on the marble. Hades' smoke flickered and Athena smiled at me and waved her hand towards the man. 'His judgment will come too, but for the moment he is safe.'

'Wait, what does that mean?' I asked her, but the commentator's voice boomed across the room.

'Well we really have been treated tonight folks, who would have thought it?' As if in response the phoenix beat its wings, moving higher above everyone. Treated? This shit-show was viewed as a treat? 'Now let's see what the judges think of Persephone's controversial actions tonight. Radamanthus?'

'Two tokens,' the chubby judge smiled at me.

'Aeacus?'

'Zero tokens,' Aeacus said, his blue skin reflecting the soft torchlight in the room.

'Minos?' The piercing look the wise man gave me was totally lost on me. I just gaped back at him, doing my best to contain the roiling emotion tearing my insides apart.

'You broke the rules, Persephone. You saved your friend.'

'That's not his fault, please don't punish him,' I whispered.

'We will not. You have shown loyalty. And that is valued higher than hospitality.' He gazed at me a second longer, then spoke.

'Two tokens.'

A box appeared in front of me, the lid open. It was the seed box, and inside were another two pomegranate seeds. I stared down at them, then back up at the judges. How could they not see that these didn't matter? I'd just stabbed a man who had accused me murdering his wife, and these maniacs were handing out fucking pomegranate seeds?

'Give me my memories back,' I said, my voice louder and clearer than I expected.

Minos gave me a small smile, and the three judges faded away.

'There you have it folks! It's the end of Round One of the Hades Trials and Persephone is not only still alive, but she has more tokens than the current leader did at the end of her first round. Who would have guessed! We'll be visiting a new realm for Round Two, and I know you're going to love it!' The commentator vanished and Athena stepped forward.

'Hades, you may deal with your intruder.'

'Wait-' I started to say, but suddenly the temperature plummeted and I was skidding across the room on my knees, along with everything else in Hades' path.

Pure terror gripped me as swirling smoke moved towards the injured man. Screaming started in the back of mind and the now familiar smell of blood filled my nostrils, churning my already empty stomach.

'Stop!' I tried to cry the word but nothing came out. I was pinned against the wall of the ballroom, and tears spilled from my eyes as Hades reached the bleeding man. With a hiss, he threw his smoky arms in the air, and the man flew up, blood spraying from his wound. My skin was so cold I could hardly feel it, and I was vaguely aware that everyone else in the room was shrinking away, melting into the walls as best they could. Everyone except Hecate.

'Hades-' she called, but the King of the Underworld roared, and the man screamed.

'You dare enter my realm, and try to kill her?' His

voice carried so much power, so much terror, so much danger, that my limbs collapsed. 'You dare to try to take her from me?' The man whimpered as he hovered in the air, and black spots danced in front of my eyes as the screaming in my head grew louder, and flames began to obscure my vision.

'Please,' I said, but the word didn't make a sound. There was a cracking noise, and the world swam as the man shrieked in pain. His arms and legs went completely taut, then began to pull away from his torso. Nausea rolled through me, followed swiftly by dizziness so intense my head lolled to one side.

'Hades, stop!' It was Hecate's voice, but I couldn't see her any more. I could only see the man I'd almost killed, and fire.

'She deserves to die,' croaked the man's hoarse voice, and black erupted through the room. In slow motion, I watched as the man's body exploded, his head and limbs flying through the air, blood spraying the very solid form of Hades. But it wasn't the Hades I'd thrown myself at that evening. This... this was something that would haunt my nightmares as long as I lived. Massive and hulking, the monster before me had onyx, soulless eyes, and as I stared, blue waves of light rolled off his enormous armor-covered body, solidifying on the ground as corpses. Corpses that were burning. Corpses that were screaming.

I couldn't breathe. *I didn't deserve to breathe.* Fear like I'd never, ever known was crushing me to death, and I deserved it. I had to die.

~

'Well, I'd hoped to see you here.'

I blinked as I looked around the garden, the Atlas fountain trickling pleasantly before me, and birdsong warming my cold skin.

'I thought I only came here when I was asleep?' I asked mildly. It was impossible to be anything but mild in this place.

'Unconscious counts as well, my dear.' I tilted my head, then dropped to my knees and ran my fingers around a budding young crocus. 'You do not have long before Hades' rage kills you, Persephone. There is only one way you may survive.'

'Did I kill that man's wife?,' I asked the voice.

'Eat the seeds, Persephone.'

A jolt like lightning shot through my body and I opened my eyes with a jerk. I was back in the ballroom, surrounded by blood and fire and bodies. Screaming so loud it drowned out my own thoughts swamped my mind, and all I could see through my stinging eyes was death.

'Persephone!' shouted a voice. 'Hades, you're going to kill her!'

I forced my eyes closed, so I didn't have to look at the bodies around me. Was I a murderer? I couldn't organize the thoughts, couldn't make sense of anything through my paralyzed fear.

Eat the seeds.

Would eating the seeds make this stop? I opened my

streaming eyes a crack, and fumbled at the floor, recoiling as I knocked the little wooden box skidding though slick blood.

Eat the seeds.

I snatched at the box, my fingers numb and shaking as the screaming got so loud I thought my head would explode. Tipping the lid open with a snap, I scooped up a pomegranate seed, and clumsily forced my hand to my lips.

Eat the seeds.

The sharpness made me gag, but I closed my eyes and took a breath through my nose, the metallic scent of blood almost making me retch again. With an effort, I swallowed the tiny seed.

The fear receded instantly, my body going completely limp as I collapsed to the cold floor. The screaming faded away, replaced by Hecate's voice, loud and shrill.

'Hades, you've fucking killed her, stop! You have to stop.'

An unbelievably peaceful calm spread through me, and I felt all of my exhausted muscles relax. This was it. This was the end. And it was surprisingly more comfortable than I thought it would be.

Something fluttered in my stomach. Then it fluttered up to my chest. I felt my body jerk as my heart responded to it. Once. Twice. A third time. Then light, green and vibrant filled my vision and something incredible flooded through my veins, sending pulsing energy to every part of my failing body. Something rich and strong and fierce. Something alien and familiar all at once.

It was power. I had my power back.

THANKS FOR READING!

Thank you so much for reading The Power of Hades, I hope you enjoyed it! If so I would be very grateful for a review! They help so much; just click here and leave a couple worlds, and you'll make my day :)

You can order the next book, The Passion of Hades, here.

You can also get exclusive first looks at artwork and story ideas, plus free short stories and audiobooks if you sign up to my newsletter at elizaraine.com.